She wakened suddenly to
gold from Resaldar's ta~~~
open and very blue and f~~~
He moved suddenly and ~~~
violence of passion and despair and desire which denied
the angry resentment with which he had suffered her
company through the mountains.

Quite abruptly he jerked away from her. 'I knew it
would be torment if you came with me,' he said tonelessly. 'And I was right.'

She was still shaken by her own primitive desires
evoked by his kiss. 'Resaldar—is there no way out? *No
way at all?*'

'There is a way.' He uttered a laugh which was completely devoid of humour or mirth. 'But I doubt if you
would be prepared to take it. It would mean destroying
your creed, your faith, and your culture.'

'I don't understand—'

'If you and I were both to convert to Islam, I would not
have to make a choice.'

'Convert to Islam?' Bella echoed in a dazed voice.
'What difference would that—'

'It would,' he answered her half-formed question
flatly, 'mean that I could then marry both Fawzia *and*
yourself.'

Born of Afrikaans-speaking parents in Johannesburg, South Africa, Christina Laffeaty describes her education as 'erratic'. Between the ages of seven and fifteen she attended twelve different schools where her attendance depended on whether or not she was needed to help out with the ploughing or harvesting! She attributes the fact that she acquired any kind of education at all to her own obsessive reading.

She was nineteen before she learned English—from her husband, who brought her to live in England—and she started writing professionally shortly afterwards. Her work includes short stories for the BBC, the *Evening News* and various women's magazines; radio plays, serials and about sixty books. Mrs Laffeaty has a son and a daughter and lives in the West Country. THE KHAN OF SHAPOORA is her fifth Masquerade Historical Romance.

THE KHAN OF SHAPOORA

CHRISTINA LAFFEATY

MILLS & BOON LIMITED
15–16 BROOK'S MEWS
LONDON W1A 1DR

First published in Great Britain 1984
by Robert Hale Limited, Clerkenwell House,
Clerkenwell Green, London ECIR 0HT

This revised and expanded edition published 1985 by
Mills & Boon Limited

© Christina Laffeaty 1984, 1985

Australian copyright 1985
Philippine copyright 1985

ISBN 0 263 75098 1

Set in 10 on 11½ pt Linotron Times
04–0585–64,300

Photoset by Rowland Phototypesetting Ltd
Bury St Edmunds, Suffolk
Made and printed in Great Britain by
Cox & Wyman Ltd, Reading

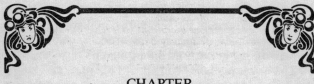

CHAPTER
ONE

NOTHING could have demonstrated Great-Uncle Howard's unpopularity more tellingly than the poor turn-out at his funeral.

Apart from a few of the older servants, who perhaps remembered him before he became a bitter old man with a grudge against life, only Bella and Simon were at the graveside. Even Mr Munday, the family solicitor, had found an excuse to stay away from the ceremony.

Bella, her hand on her young brother's arm, turned away from the grave. A sad, dreary sifting of rain blurred the Sussex landscape, and they hurried to gain the shelter of the waiting carriage with its black-plumed horses. As they drove back to Haverington Hall Bella could not help remembering the first time she had entered by the imposing iron gates and travelled along the sweeping tree-lined drive towards the house.

That had been six years ago, in 1873. She had been eighteen, and Simon a little boy of eleven. Their parents had been killed in a train accident, leaving them penniless, and there had been no one but Great-Uncle Howard to take them in.

Bella remembered his late wife, Great-Aunt Sophie, as a frightened, defeated woman who had probably been grateful to escape from her marriage by dying at an early age. Great-Uncle Howard had never sought to replace her with some other unfortunate female, which was perhaps the only unselfish demonstration in his entire life.

Bella's heart could still jerk with humiliation and pain as she remembered the graceless, grudging way in which he had offered herself and Simon a home.

'The boy is my heir,' he had said bluntly. 'There's no one else left to inherit Haverington Hall. So, I have a duty to feed and clothe and educate him. He'll go to Eton. As for yourself—'

He had given her a cruel, analytical glance. 'You have neither looks nor fortune. You'll die an old maid. You might as well learn how to earn your keep, therefore.'

She had more than earned her keep during the past six years. Great-Uncle Howard had exploited her mercilessly, kept her at his beck and call, and constantly reminded her that she was beholden to him for the very food she was eating. For Simon's sake she had quelled her rebellious spirit. If it had not been for her brother, Bella would long ago have left and sought employment somewhere as a housekeeper or a companion.

She sighed. No, it would be hypocritical to pretend that she grieved for her aged relative. She was only sorry that he had made so many enemies, that he had lived for seventy years without apparently enriching the life of a single other human being.

Bella caught her brother's gaze upon her, and smiled. So many things would alter for the better now that Simon was to inherit Haverington Hall.

The carriage had drawn up outside the house. 'I'm starving!' Simon announced.

'The servants will be bringing refreshments to the drawing room presently.' Bella gave her brother an affectionate push towards the door. 'Go and entertain Mr Munday while I remove my bonnet.'

In the hall, before entering the drawing-room, Bella stood in front of a hanging mirror while she removed the black crêpe bonnet from her head. It had been the only item of mourning wear which she had been able to buy for the old man's funeral, and for that she had had to raid the housekeeping money. Otherwise, she had improvised by sewing a mourning fringe around the edge of her best gown of serviceable grey serge.

She studied her reflection in the mirror for a moment. How sick she was of serviceable gowns in drab colours! They swamped her personality, drained the colour from her grey-green eyes and did nothing to bring out the auburn tints in her brown hair. Of course she looked every bit as plain as Great-Uncle Howard had always tauntingly claimed. She had never had a chance to look anything but plain. Who would notice that her figure was slim-waisted and well proportioned, always obscured as it was by dreary ill-made house-gowns? If only—

Bella sighed, commonsense reasserting itself. There was no point in fanciful dreaming. She had to face facts. Her future lay mapped out before her and there was not a thing she could do to change her destiny.

She would keep house at Haverington Hall for Simon until he married. And then—well, she could only hope that there might still be a place for her somewhere in his life, perhaps as a doting maiden aunt to his children, a companion to his wife, an uncomplaining and self-effacing drudge, coping with unpleasant domestic chores. That, after all, was the lot of most penniless spinsters.

She shrugged, and made her way to the drawing room where Simon and Mr Munday were waiting for her. The solicitor was paging through a thick sheaf of papers; when he saw her he placed them on a table, and rose to meet her.

'Ah, Arabella! I am sorry, my dear, that I had to cry off from attending the funeral. My rheumatism—and the wretched rain—'

She smiled. 'Of course I understand, Mr Munday. Now, would you like to explain great-uncle's will to us before the servants bring in the refreshments, or leave it until later?'

'I think it may be as well to make a beginning.' He sat down and picked up the sheaf of papers once more. 'The will itself is quite straightforward. Simon is to get the bulk of the estate. And you, my dear—'

He cleared his throat with patent embarrassment, and reached for the will. '*To my great-niece Arabella,*' he read, '*I bequeath a sum equal to the figure of twenty pounds for each year she has spent at Haverington Hall. Twenty pounds per annum is, I understand, the normal wage for upper servants, and is no more nor less than she has a right to expect.*'

Bella flushed with angry mortification. How typical of Great-Uncle Howard to arrange for his malice and vindictiveness to reach out even from beyond the grave! Then she forced a lightness in her tone. 'A total of one hundred and twenty pounds! It is more than I have ever expected to possess at one time in my life.'

Mr Munday inclined his head. 'And it is to be paid to you whatever happens, while Simon's inheritance is wholly tied up with the entire estate.'

'*Whatever happens*—' Bella echoed sharply. 'The matter is quite clear-cut, is it not? Simon gets the bulk of the money and the estate?'

'There is the entail—' Mr Munday began.

'The entail, as I understood it, is broken as soon as there is no direct Haverington descendant. Simon is not a Haverington, and therefore there is no longer an entail on the estate!'

'Arabella,' Mr Munday said quietly, 'I am afraid there is the most wretched of complications. You will remember that I cleared your great-uncle's desk after his death, and took away with me all his documents so that I could deal with any outstanding matters.'

Bella nodded tensely, steeling herself. Whatever complications could there possibly be? Simon, characteristically, seemed more concerned with the food which the servants had begun to carry into the room.

When the three of them were once more alone, Mr Munday went on. 'There is a hidden drawer in your great-uncle's desk. But for the fact that I own a desk designed by the same cabinet-maker, I would never have known about its existence, and neither would I automatically have opened it when I cleared the desk.'

'You found something in the hidden drawer?'

The lawyer nodded unhappily. 'It's my belief that Mr Haverington did not wish it to be found until the matter had become ancient history. He could not bring himself to destroy it, and so he buried it instead in a place where he hoped it might remain undisturbed for generations.'

'What *was* it, Mr Munday?' Bella demanded.

Carefully, the solicitor selected a sheet of paper from the documents before him and handed it to Bella. The ink was faded, the writing so compressed and crossed that it was impossible to make out more than one or two words.

'I can't read this,' Bella said, frowning. She handed the paper back to Mr Munday. 'What does it mean?'

'What do you know about Jack Haverington?' the lawyer demanded unexpectedly in return.

'Great-Uncle Howard's son? Why, only that he died tragically at the age of eighteen in India, soon after he had been bought a commission as a junior officer in the Army—'

'That was the story that was put about,' Mr Munday corrected. 'The truth was rather less honourable. Jack Haverington was a wild young man who had been

expelled from school. At seventeen he was running up
gambling debts in London. A year later his father, at his
wits' end, got him into the Army and Jack went to India
with his regiment. Shortly afterwards he deserted, and
nothing was ever heard from him again. Until *this*—' he
indicated the sheet of paper.

'Are you saying that *Jack Haverington* wrote it?' Bella
asked sharply.

'No. It was written by a missionary in Afghanistan. It
is undated, and as you saw it is almost impossible to
decipher with the naked eye. It took me several days,
with the aid of a magnifying glass, to make out what it
says. Since I know it almost by heart now, I had better
read it to you.'

Mr Munday cleared his throat.'*Dear Mr Haverington,*' he began. '*I am writing to you on behalf of your son
Jack, whom I met about a year ago and who I now
understand finds himself in a situation from which only
you could possibly rescue him.*

'*You will have been told, I daresay, that he deserted his
regiment. He explained the circumstances to me and I feel
it only right that I should make you cognizant of them too.*

'*In 1852 his company was stationed with a small garrison at Lucknow. Things had been tense for some time; the
sepoys were openly hostile to the British officers, and
there was an atmosphere of simmering hatred against
them. The few British officers were hopelessly outnumbered by the Indian sepoys in the garrison, and Jack at the
tender age of eighteen felt particularly vulnerable. Things
became very much worse after three of the sepoys had to
be executed following a mutinous incident in the garrison.*

'*In that tense atmosphere, the British officers received
orders that they were to march towards Rangoon as war
had been declared against the King of Burma. The
thought of that long march, accompanied by overwhelm-*

ing numbers of resentful, hate-filled sepoys, was too much for Jack, and he deserted.'

Mr Munday paused to sip from his sherry glass. '*I do not have space,*' he continued, '*for a detailed account of your son's flight from India. Suffice it to say that he eventually found himself in Kabul, where he succeeded in installing himself as tutor to the sons of Shere Ali, the Emir of Kabul.*

'*As fate would have it, he fell in love with one of the Emir's daughters, Shazeen, and she with him. In spite of the strict regime prevailing at the palace they contrived to meet, and, to cut a long and reprehensible story short, she found that she was expecting Jack's child. It became necessary for them to flee, as they would otherwise have been beheaded by the Emir.*'

Simon had been paying fascinated attention to the letter. 'Why,' he broke in, 'couldn't they have thrown themselves on the Emir's mercy? After all, Shazeen was his *daughter*!'

Mr Munday shook his head. 'What they did offended against Islamic law and could not be forgiven. They would have had to die.' He resumed reading again.

'*Jack and Shazeen ran away together, into the mountains. They lived in an old Buddhist cave which they discovered, existing from hand to mouth, sometimes helped by wandering tribesmen or travellers. I was one of those travellers, and that is how I came to be acquainted with your son's history.*

'*After I left the cave I went on to do missionary work near Jellalabad, and it is only recently that I received a report which disturbs me greatly, and which has prompted me to write to you.*

'*I have learnt that your son, together with Shazeen and their infant boy Resaldar, were captured by a band of marauding nomads and taken into the Sulaiman Mountains where the nomads have a stronghold called Shapoora.*

'*The tribe are known as Kaffirs or Infidels. They are exiles from the Hindu Kush who have been used to living in savage freedom for generations, and they acknowledge allegiance to no one. They are as desperate, as dangerous a tribe of brigands as one could hope to meet, and they live by plundering travellers along the Khyber Pass, or by kidnapping and holding to ransom important members of other tribes.*

'*My informants tell me that the Infidels do not know the identity of your son or of Shazeen, but they have guessed that she is of noble birth, and they keep the young family alive in the hope of some day being able to extract a ransom for them. In the meantime they exist as virtual slaves to the Infidels.*

'*Since I regard the story which Jack told me about himself in the same light as a secret of the confessional, I cannot go to the authorities. Besides, Jack is still wanted for desertion by the British Army, and the Emir would undoubtedly have all three of them killed if his aid were sought.*

'*You are the only one who could conceivably help to free the three prisoners, perhaps by means of a privately financed body of mercenaries. I can do no more than leave the matter in your hands. I remain, sir, your obedient servant, Reverend Percy Dawkes.*'

Mr Munday laid the letter down.

'What an abominable man Great-Uncle Howard was!' Bella exclaimed. 'He simply locked the letter away in a secret drawer and did nothing!'

'I suppose he couldn't forgive Jack.' Mr Munday peered at them over his spectacles. 'You understand the implications of the letter, do you not? If Jack Haverington is still alive, then by the terms of the entail Haverington Hall has to pass to him and not to Simon.'

'I hope he is still alive!' Simon burst out. 'What a monstrous story! How could Great-Uncle Howard have left the estate to me, knowing that his own son might still be rotting among a band of savages!'

Bella was chewing at her lip. 'You said the letter was undated. Is there any indication as to when it was written?'

Mr Munday stared at it in a considering way. 'I checked with church records, and discovered that the Reverend Percy Dawkes died in Jellalabad ten years ago. The fact that he did not write to Mr Haverington again suggests that the letter was penned shortly before his death. It fits in with other facts too. About ten years ago Howard Haverington suffered a slight stroke. The shock of receiving the letter could have caused it. Also, his behaviour became markedly more bitter and vindictive towards mankind at about that time.'

'Ten years ago . . .' Bella echoed. 'All that time, living in slavery, at the mercy of a tribe of brigands . . . Great-Uncle Howard must surely have been the most unspeakable man who ever drew breath!'

'I wonder if they are still alive,' Simon mused. 'We must do something to find out, and rescue them if they are. What *can* be done, Mr Munday?'

'Very little, I'm afraid. We can't go to the authorities, for Jack Haverington deserted in war-time. He could still be shot.'

'Surely they wouldn't shoot an old man?' Simon cried, outraged.

'Jack would be no more than forty-seven now,' the lawyer pointed out. 'And I don't see how the British Army could possibly spare his life if he were found. We are at war with Afghanistan, and the Army could hardly pardon him without encouraging others who might be considering desertion.'

Bella frowned thoughtfully at Mr Munday. 'I suppose, as executor of the estate, you will not authorise the hiring of mercenaries, as the missionary suggested in his letter?'

'I could not possibly do such a thing at a time when our armed forces are already engaged in Afghanistan.'

'But the three of them *must* be rescued if they are still alive! Mr Munday, even apart from the humanity of the issue, you must surely see that something must be done to rescue them, or at least establish whether they are alive or not? For one thing, what would our legal and financial position be while we continue in this state of limbo?'

'Precarious, to say the least,' the lawyer admitted. 'Mr Haverington left little in actual cash; the estate's income is solely derived from the various farms, and rents paid on properties in Haverington Village. All that will have to be frozen from now on. And I'm afraid I couldn't authorise the continued payment of Simon's school fees out of the estate. I confess that matters are bleak for both of you.

'The house will have to be closed and the servants dismissed. I could stretch a point, Arabella, and employ you as caretaker here, which would at least give you and Simon a roof over your heads—'

'With Haverington Hall gradually mouldering away around us,' she interrupted sharply, 'and Simon's education blighted! We *cannot* continue indefinitely in such a state! Something must be done to settle the issue one way or another!'

Mr Munday hesitated. 'One solution which did occur to me was that a sympathetic British officer garrisoned in Afghanistan might be persuaded to make an unauthorised raid on this Shapoora, and discreetly effect a rescue if the prisoners are still alive. Indeed, my own nephew

Charles is in Afghanistan with his regiment, and might be influenced to make such a raid . . .'

'Could you write and ask him?' Bella demanded eagerly.

The lawyer shook his head. 'I could not possibly put such a request in writing. If it fell into the wrong hands, it could prove disastrous.'

'Yes, I see . . . Will you have a chance of speaking to him in the near future?'

'Unfortunately not. He is not due to receive home leave for some time.'

'But if someone could travel to Afghanistan,' Bella persisted, 'and plead for his help—'

Mr Munday spread his hands. 'I can think of no one who could be trusted with such a delicate mission.'

Bella was silent for a long while. At last, squaring her shoulders, she demanded, 'Would it cost more than a hundred and twenty pounds to travel to Afghanistan, Mr Munday?'

'I don't believe so, but—'

'I'll go with you!' Simon cried, following his sister's thoughts.

'No, you won't,' Bella said firmly.

'It isn't fair—'

'The thing is impossible!' Mr Munday silenced both of them. 'It's out of the question for you to travel to Afghanistan, Arabella!'

'Who else *is* there, Mr Munday? No one!'

'We are at war with Afghanistan—'

'Precisely! And almost daily the wives and servants of officers garrisoned at Jellalabad and Peshawar leave for that country! Who knows what might happen after the war is over? It might be impossible for any Briton to travel to the Sulaiman Mountains by then. Now is precisely the time for me to go there!'

'It would be quite improper,' Mr Munday protested. 'A young woman, alone and unchaperoned—'

'I'm twenty-four,' she told the lawyer, smiling. 'My great-uncle never missed an opportunity to remind me that I am an old maid. The one compensation which being an old maid brings is that one no longer has to fret so much about the proprieties. So, if you would kindly write an introduction to your nephew for me, I shall arrange to travel for Afghanistan at the earliest possible opportunity!'

'And what am I supposed to do while you are away?' Simon demanded resentfully. 'I won't be able to return to Eton, because Mr Munday has said my school fees can't be paid. Am I to remain here completely alone, without even servants for company?'

'I'm sure the Ransomes would allow you to stay with them—'

'I hate the Ransomes!'

Mr Munday had remained thoughtfully silent during their argument. 'The boy is right,' he said unexpectedly. 'If you are to go, Arabella, then he must accompany you. There is safety in numbers.'

'You've changed your mind? You agree that I should go?'

'Reluctantly, yes. What you have said is quite true; there *is* no one else who could be entrusted with a message to my nephew, and you are a sensible, dependable girl. Also it is impossible to predict the outcome of the war; if we lost, the frontier might be closed to all Britishers, and then we would have to go on in this state of uncertainty regarding the inheritance, with no hope of resolving the matter, perhaps for ever.'

'How are we to travel to Afghanistan?' Simon asked eagerly.

Mr Munday was thoughtful for a moment. 'I shall

have to approach the proper Army channels and arrange for you to travel in company with the next group of officers' wives bound for Jellalabad. Your expenses will, of course, be paid by the estate. Arabella, you had best start packing so that you may be ready to leave at short notice.'

Bella lost no time, after he had gone, in obeying the lawyer's instructions. Simon's packing occupied more of her time than did her own, simply because he possessed more clothes than she did.

She shook her head ruefully as she surveyed her wardrobe of serviceable gowns, and could only hope that they would suffice. It had not occurred to Mr Munday that she might need new clothes, and she had not liked to bring the subject up. But in spite of the meagreness of her wardrobe, and in spite of the underlying seriousness of the reasons for their mission, Bella could not help enjoying the prospect of travelling to a far-away place and of encountering the unfamiliar.

She, who had never expected life to have anything more in store for her than domestic drudgery, was on the threshold of an exciting venture.

Mr Munday called on them again a few days later. 'Everything has been arranged,' he said. 'I shall drive you to the station where you are to join a large contingent of Army wives, servants and other camp followers. If you are ready, let us leave as soon as possible. We shall have to put up in a London hostelry for the night.'

It did not take long for the luggage to be stowed aboard Mr Munday's carriage, and after last-minute instructions to the servants they set off on the first leg of their journey.

That evening, while they were dining in the parlour of a London inn, Mr Munday handed Bella a letter addressed to his nephew Charles. 'When you reach

Bombay,' he told her, 'you will be given a military escort to Jellalabad.'

Merely being in London, with its gas lights and its vibrant raucousness was exciting enough; when Bella looked at Simon she saw that her brother shared her feeling of awed anticipation at the prospect of visiting such exotic locations as Bombay and Jellalabad.

She slept little that night, and it was not only the noise of the London streets which kept her awake. There was so much to think about; the long journey ahead of them which, however exciting it might be, would almost certainly be arduous as well. And then there was the question of whether or not they would be able to find and rescue Jack Haverington and his wife and son.

After breakfast the next morning Mr Munday drove them to the railway station to board the train for Dover. A large crowd milled about on the platform and it was immediately obvious that they were all bound for the same destination. Apart from a few officers and what were obviously servants the vast majority of passengers boarding the train were women, and Bella was relieved to see that her own plain travelling gown of dark-blue oatmeal-cloth did not form too sharp a contrast with those worn by many of the other women.

Mr Munday kissed Bella's cheeks and shook hands with Simon and a little later the train steamed out of the station.

The journey to Dover, and the Channel crossing, became slightly tedious once the initial novelty had worn off. It was only when they reached Brindisi in Italy where they were to board the P & O liner that Bella and Simon felt their real journey was about to begin.

Brindisi itself was remarkable only for its dirt and its many beggars. On the quay, ragged urchins vied anxiously with one another for the chance of earning a little money by darting for any item of luggage they could see in order to carry it on board the waiting vessel. Laughing, Simon drew Bella's attention to the startling sight of two Englishwomen who, having mistaken the motives of the urchins, were brandishing their husbands' sabres at the children and forcing the bewildered urchins to drop the portmanteaux they had picked up.

Soon all the luggage had been safely stowed and the passengers boarded. One of the young women among them drew Bella's particular attention. She was extremely beautiful in an expensively groomed way, with elaborate golden curls and blue eyes, and she was accompanied by a retinue of servants who were carrying a great deal of luggage.

She caught Bella's interested gaze upon her and returned it with a long, arrogant stare. She did not appear on deck after the first day, so presumably she suffered from sea-sickness and kept to her cabin.

Bella dismissed the golden-haired, haughty stranger from her mind, and she and Simon settled down to enjoy the voyage. Unlike most of the other passengers, who declared themselves to be thoroughly bored after the first week at sea, Bella and her young brother savoured every moment of every day.

The food was excellent and plentiful, and there was always something with which to occupy one's time. The military section on board organised a series of walking matches, and each day at noon there was the thrill and the excitement of watching the log being heaved.

The log was a triangular piece of wood which remained stationary when thrown out to sea. It was attached to a line wound over a reel, and according to the amount of line paid out in a given number of seconds the speed of the vessel could be calculated. Passengers streamed after the quarter-master and his aides as they marched aft with the reel and a minute-glass, and small sums were wagered on the number of knots the vessel was travelling.

There were other diversions too. Bella was disappointed that the liner would be arriving in Suez during the night, but she found that the moon in those parts shone with a light which equalled that of London's gas-lamps, so that she was able to catch at least a glimpse of a small part of Egypt.

Even when there were no such diversions, she and Simon enjoyed the lazy pleasures of shipboard life.

'This certainly beats school!' Simon rhapsodised for the dozenth time as he flopped on deck beside Bella, gazing at the surrounding ocean. Then he became serious. 'Do you think Cousin Resaldar—if he is still alive—will be about my age?

'A few years younger, if the missionary's letter arrived ten years ago.'

'I always wanted a brother, or at the very least, a male cousin,' he said wistfully.

'Simon,' Bella warned, 'don't expect Resaldar to be like an English boy. Remember, he has spent his entire life in bondage to savages. He will probably be very timid and cowed. Also, if we are to effect the rescue of him and his parents, you must not talk about the matter in public. We must not prejudice the chances of a rescue by being indiscreet.'

He promised, and changed the subject. 'While we are in Bombay, could we visit the famous stables where the Arab horses are sold to the Army?'

'If we have time. How do you know about the stables?'

'I have read about them,' her brother told her eagerly. 'The horses are brought from the Persian Gulf to Bombay, and kept in stables there.'

Bella smiled at her horse-mad brother, 'As I've said, we'll visit the stables if we have time. But we must not risk being left behind in Bombay when the rest of the passengers leave with the military escort.'

Bombay itself came as a surprise to Bella. She had not expected it to be quite so British in character. And yet, when she thought about it and remembered the history books she had read, she realised that the business capital of the province was entirely a British creation, sovereignty over its possession having been part of the dowry which Catherine of Braganza had bestowed on the British monarch she was to marry.

But the heterogeneous races who made up the city's population more than cancelled out the British architecture of most of the buildings. Apart from the British officers with their scarlet and blue, there were men in colourful robes and women draped in saris, and a babel of different tongues assaulted one's ears.

The passengers dispersed to their different hotels in accordance with their means. Bella and Simon, in company with the wives of several junior officers, were billeted in what was clearly meant to be a fairly modest establishment but which to Bella seemed quite opulent.

She learnt from the officers' wives that they were to spend two nights in Bombay before taking the train to the railhead. Simon grinned at her; he would have a chance to see the stables of the Arab horses after all.

That evening, in the dining room of their hotel, Bella was struggling to cope with an unfamiliar fruit when she looked up to find a pair of amused brown eyes regarding her.

The man smiled. He was in his early thirties, perhaps, with a pleasantly craggy face and dark hair. When Bella returned his smile he rose and approached their table.

'It's called a mango, ma'am,' he said, indicating the

fruit, 'and not really fit for eating in polite company, being somewhat messy. I should content myself with the grapes if I were you.'

Within a short while he had joined them, and the three of them were deep in conversation. The stranger's name was Lionel Bromley, and he was a war correspondent for a British newspaper. He had arrived a day or two earlier from Jellalabad to collect photographic equipment which had been shipped out from England. His manner was so easy and sympathetic that Bella found herself relaxing in his company.

'And which officer's household are you and your brother joining, Miss Stanley?' he wanted to know.

'Well—' She hesitated. 'Major Charles Munday's, actually—'

To her discomfiture, he pursued the subject. 'Are you related to him? I saw him recently, and he did not mention that he was expecting visitors from England.'

Simon came to her rescue by changing the subject deliberately. 'Mr Bromley, do you know where the stables are located in which the Arab horses are sold?'

'Indeed I do.'

'We wish to visit them tomorrow. If you could, perhaps, sketch a map for us—'

'I shall do better than that! I shall escort you there myself tomorrow after breakfast.'

The conversation became concentrated upon horses after that, and Lionel Bromley asked no further awkward questions.

True to his word, he escorted them to the famous stables the following morning. It was a picturesque sight, the bright colours worn by the Arab traders contrasting with the dusty and rather sombre appearance of the stables themselves.

Bella did not quite share the passionate interest of her

brother in the horses, and once she had expressed her admiration for their beauty she contented herself with studying the Arab owners of the horses who were sitting on the seats outside the stables, smoking and drinking coffee. It seemed to her a very long way to travel in order to sell horses.

When Simon had seen everything he wished to, they returned to the hotel in time for lunch. The heat was oppressive, and since Lionel Bromley was to spend the afternoon in supervising the unloading of his photographic equipment from the liner and could not escort them around the city, Bella decided to rest in her room, and firmly ordered Simon to do so as well. 'We shall have to get up very early tomorrow,' she told him, 'in order to catch the train to the railhead.'

At dinner that evening Lionel Bromley joined them as a matter of course, and to Bella's dismay he returned to the subject of her visit to Jellalabad to stay with Major Charles Munday.

After hedging desperately for a while, she decided to trust him. He listened carefully as she confided the whole story to him, and when she came to the end of it he shook his head very definitely.

'Charles Munday would be the last person in whom to entrust such a tale!'

'But why, Mr Bromley? His uncle said—'

'I don't know how long it is since his uncle last saw him, but Munday is a stickler for Army rules. And he certainly wouldn't risk his career for something like this. No, he would report immediately to his superiors if you appealed to him with your story.'

'I can't simply return to England,' Bella said with dismay, 'and leave those three wretched people to their fate, with our own positions unresolved for years to come!'

'No, indeed.' Lionel Bromley's eyes glowed with

professional excitement. 'The rescue of this little family would make a first-class story for the readers of my newspaper, and so I propose to help you, Miss Stanley.'

'The last thing Jack Haverington can afford is publicity!' she objected. 'If he *were* found, he would have to assume a new identity. He and Shazeen and Resaldar would have to come to Haverington Hall, ostensibly as distant relations of ours, and Jack will probably have to assume control of the estate in the guise of Simon's guardian. All those complicated details have yet to be worked out. But in the meantime, the utmost discretion must be maintained!'

'You may rely on me to be discreet, Miss Stanley. I shall not identify the three of them if I write about them, I give you my word.'

'But what could you possibly do to help?' Bella asked dubiously.

'More than you imagine. I am friendly with one or two of the Khans. I'll make enquiries about this village stronghold, Shapoora, and once we have established where it is I'll bribe the Khans to mount a raid on it.'

'Who,' Simon interrupted, wide-eyed, 'are the Khans, Mr Bromley?'

'The word Khan is a title. It means chief, ruler, prince. Afghanistan is split into numerous tribes, each with its own Khan.'

Bella said resignedly, 'I suppose I have no alternative but to put the matter in your hands, and to thank you.'

Lionel Bromley nodded, and said briskly, 'If we are to ask the Khans for help, we cannot travel with the military. It would frighten them off. There are two trains to the railhead tomorrow. The Army wives will take the first; we shall wait and catch the second.'

'Shall we be safe without a military escort?' Bella asked anxiously.

'Quite safe. I shall hire a caravan of armed guards at the railhead. The only suggestion I would make is that—well, forgive me, but you look to be roughly of a size with your brother, and I would be happier if you could borrow some of his clothing for the journey. As two youths, you would be less conspicuous than as a young lady and a boy travelling with me. Not,' he hastened to add, 'that I expect any danger, but it would be a prudent precaution.'

Much later that evening, after he had excused himself and left them, Simon asked gravely, 'Do you trust Mr Bromley, Bella?'

'Yes, I think so. He seems genuine, and it's obvious that he knows Afghanistan well.'

'I trust him too.' Simon grinned. 'What a jape—you dressing up as a boy! You're not having my best breeches, mind!'

At noon the next day, Bella and Simon were waiting with Lionel Bromley to board the train to the railhead. Bella, clad in a shirt and breeches borrowed from Simon and with her hair pinned up underneath a sturdy sun helmet, looked convincingly like a rather delicate youth. She was listening tolerantly to her brother's jokes about her appearance when they became aware of a furious exchange taking place inside the station-master's office.

'It's quite outrageous!' a female voice exclaimed. 'Could the train not have waited for me? I was no more than half an hour late!'

'The Memsahib must understand,' an apologetic voice answered her, 'the time-table—'

'Oh, the devil take the time-table! What is half an hour here or there? And what were my servants about, that they did not insist on the engine-driver waiting? What am I to do, with all my luggage and my servants gone on ahead?'

'If the Memsahib would take the next train,' the station master suggested, 'her servants and luggage will without a doubt be waiting at the railhead.'

A short while later, just before the train steamed into the station, the owner of the angry female voice emerged from the station-master's office, and Bella was intrigued to see that it was the arrogant, golden-haired beauty she had first encountered on the liner.

Bella did not see the girl again during the train journey. Only when the train arrived at the railhead was she once more in evidence. She was weeping with fury and a touch of hysteria because her servants had not waited for her with the luggage.

'What am I to do?' the girl wailed to whoever cared to listen. 'How am I to reach Jellalabad?'

Lionel Bromley caught Bella's eye and grinned. Then he approached the girl. 'No doubt, ma'am, your servants felt obliged to leave the railhead with the other passengers, and will be waiting for you at the first *dāk* bungalow, or staging house, on the way. I am hiring a caravan to escort me and my party, and would be happy for you to travel in our company.'

'Well . . .' the girl said ungraciously. 'I suppose that will have to do. I am Miss Nicolette Prewitt.'

She did not deign to volunteer much further information about herself, beyond the fact that she was joining her father, General Prewitt.

She waited with disdainful detachment as the camels were made to lie down and baggage, provisions and other equipment was packed on their backs.

'I sincerely trust,' she remarked, 'that *I* am not expected to travel on one of these beasts!'

'Indeed not,' Bromley grinned. 'We shall travel by mail cart.'

That evening they arrived at an austere, mud-walled

building which Lionel Bromley told them was the first of the *dāk* bungalows in which they would be spending their nights.

Everything was bustle and confusion at the bungalow. While some of its servants came out to attend to the needs of the animals, others shepherded the passengers inside, and Bella caught sight of a young Indian in frantic pursuit of a chicken which she guessed was to serve for their supper.

Nicolette flew into a fury when there was no sign of her servants. Bella emerged from the functional bedroom which she was to share with Simon, and heard Bromley give it as his opinion that they must have returned to Bombay when they realised their mistress had not caught the train. Half-heartedly, he offered that she should remain with his party in the hope of meeting up with a military squad on its way to Jellalabad, and she accepted without grace.

Bella had been quite right about the chicken. It was indeed served to them in the form of a curry, and the toughness of the meat drew further complaints from Nicolette Prewitt.

After the meal, Bella drew Lionel Bromley to one side. 'Since Miss Prewitt is to accompany us, and I cannot see *her* consenting to masquerade as a boy, shall I resume wearing my own clothes?'

'I would rather you didn't. We would have to explain that you adopted boys' clothing in the first place as a precaution, and any hint of possible danger will throw her into uncontrolled panic. Besides,' he added with a grin, 'if she were to know that you are a girl I am quite sure she would try to press you into service as a lady's maid.'

'She would not have much success!' Bella responded with spirit.

'All the same, continue sharing Simon's wardrobe,

will you? *One* girl in this party is going to attract far too much attention as it is, and if I thought she might possibly pass as a youth I would force her into breeches too. Besides, you will find those breeches far more comfortable than female apparel in the conditions awaiting us.'

Bella reflected ruefully on the concern she had felt regarding her own limited wardrobe. Had she known that she would be spending the larger part of the journey in Simon's clothes it would have prevented much heart-searching. And how fortunate it was proving to be that Simon's school had forced Great-Uncle Howard to spend money on an adequate wardrobe for her brother!

As their journey continued Bella discovered that Lionel Bromley had spoken the truth when he'd said that boys' breeches would be more comfortable than a female's stays and petticoats, for she was obviously suffering far less than was Nicolette Prewitt.

Even so, the days became a blur of heat, dust and fatigue, and with one exception they were enduring the privations of their travel with grim acceptance.

Nicolette Prewitt was still with them, for they had met no military body, and she was still complaining unceasingly. Her travelling dress had become so crumpled and grimy that she had been forced to accept the offer of a sari from a woman at one of the *dāk* houses. She was mortified at having to wear it, and Bella thought guiltily of the gowns packed away in her own trunks. But then, the spoilt young woman would probably have scorned her humble wardrobe no less than she did the sari.

It afforded Bella a certain grim amusement that Nicolette had never once shown a sign of suspecting her own true sex. The fact was that the girl had no interest whatever in her fellow-travellers; she was absorbed only in bemoaning her own lot and complaining about the hardships she was being forced to endure.

When, at last, they reached the foothills of the Sulaiman Mountains in Afghanistan even Nicolette stopped her complaints, for she was stricken dumb with dismay.

Burnt grey-brown, the landscape with its sterile hills and vast snow-topped mountains and parched soil lay shimmering in the pitiless heat of the sun. Afghanistan was a stark, drab-coloured, inhospitable country.

The Khyber Pass itself turned out to be a dry, wide and winding valley between disconnected groups of mountains and hills. Now their party halted frequently while Lionel Bromley made expeditions into the mountains to consult his friends, the Khans.

He returned from these visits, more and more puzzled and troubled. 'There seems to be a conspiracy of silence surrounding Shapoora and its people,' he reported to Bella. 'It strikes me that it is a silence induced by fear. It appears that the tribe's reputation is as menacing as ever. But don't despair. I have a few more enquiries to make—'

He broke off at a squeal of terror from Nicolette Prewitt. Men dressed in brigand-like *achkans* and armed to the teeth with jezails, pistols and knives, were riding towards them from the mountains.

'Don't be alarmed,' Bromley said. 'These would be the guards who are employed to keep the Pass free from robbers—'

He was interrupted by a shot singing through the air. Clearly, what the newcomers had in mind was not protection. Bromley's guides had already sensed their menace and were taking flight. The horses, which had been unhitched from the cart, scattered in their wake.

The party of Britons could only wait, powerless against such overwhelming odds, as the villainous-looking brigands rode purposefully towards them.

CHAPTER
TWO

WITH A terrible, numb hopelessness, Bella had been expecting that they would all be killed out of hand and their possessions stolen. But the men who overcame and disarmed them seemed to have little interest in their possessions, and if they meant to kill the British party it was clearly to be done at some later stage.

Their trunks were loaded on the backs of camels, and by means of gestures the four of them were ordered to mount spare horses and ride, at gun-point, with their captors.

Almost the worst part of that nightmare ride into the mountains was the uncertainty of their eventual fate. For two days they travelled through some of the most pitiless countryside Bella had ever thought to see.

Even though their abductors never used physical harassment, and even allowed them a measure of privacy whenever they stopped to rest, the ever-present menace of their guns and the wildness of the country they were entering cast Bella into a turmoil of fear and despair. But even greater was her sense of guilt at what she had brought her young brother to. She wished that she, too, could give vent to her feelings by weeping and raging in turn, as Nicolette Prewitt was doing. But apart from the fact that it was not in her nature to abandon self-control, she reasoned that it would be safer to hide her sex for as long as possible from their captors.

At last their surroundings became less bleak. A beautiful tamarisk flowered near an ancient wall, and deeply-shadowing trees began to mark their way. After crossing a precipitous watercourse they began to ascend an eminence on which a village stood guarded by a cluster of trees.

Their captors entered with them through a door in the mud wall of the village and led them into a garden. Now, at last, they were able to dismount. A terrace overlooked the river, Bella saw, and in the shade of a fig-tree small carpets and cushions were invitingly scattered.

But they were made to enter a building of sun-baked brick with a watch-tower and loopholes, and ordered to climb the stairs to an upper storey.

A door was thrown open. Their captors salaamed to an unseen presence inside the room, and beckoned to them to enter.

The room was dominated by a man seated on a carved charpoy. He was gazing intently at a chess-board in front of him, his chin cupped in his hand, an arrogant tilt to his head. He wore a voluminous loose turban of rich silk wound several times about his head, and culminating in a swathe of material which fell over his left shoulder and cast his face in shadow.

Then he glanced up at the prisoners, and Bella caught her breath in surprise, for he was young—perhaps two or three years older than herself. The loosely fitting turban had shifted slightly, revealing not the black locks she would have expected but curls the warm, tawny colour of honey. His face, clean-shaven and darkened by the sun to a shade deeper than his hair, was strong, with regular features. His eyes were the biggest shock of all in that Afghan village. Set beneath dark brows and fringed by long, straight lashes, they were a clear, vivid blue.

He rose, and now Bella saw that he was tall. He wore an embroidered tunic over long, loose white robes and his feet were thrust into sandals. He was regarding them with a saturnine expression.

'So,' he said at last in clear, unaccented English. 'My spies tell me that you have been displaying an unhealthy interest in my village.'

'Your village?' Lionel Bromley exclaimed, astonished. 'This is Shapoora? Then you must be—'

'Resaldar,' the blue-eyed man acknowledged regally. 'The Khan of Shapoora. That is who I am, of course.'

After the first few moments of disbelief and shock, Bella exchanged blank glances with Simon and Lionel Bromley. All her preconceived notions had been overturned, and she felt completely disoriented.

The Khan of Shapoora . . . A Khan was a chief or a prince, and indeed Resaldar's appearance and his haughty arrogance proclaimed him to be the overlord of these mountain tribesmen. But if he was indeed their second cousin, then that letter from the missionary to Great-Uncle Howard must have been written considerably longer ago than ten years. Besides, the letter had made it clear that the captives were being kept in virtual slavery by the Infidels. How, then, could Resaldar possibly have grown up to be their chief?

But Simon clearly had no reservations. 'Why, Cou—' he began eagerly.

Swiftly, Bella dug her fingers into his arm so that he stopped and yelped with pain. Instinct told her that they should tread warily. Nothing was as they had expected it to be.

Resaldar clapped his hands, summoning the two salaaming tribesmen who stood guard outside the door.

He spoke to them for some minutes in an unintelligible tongue.

'This is all your fault, Mr Bromley!' Nicolette Prewitt burst out suddenly, with hysteria in her voice. 'You were supposed to protect me—'

'Nothing calamitous has happened to you yet,' he pointed out soothingly, 'and I daresay nothing will, provided you control your tongue. If this man is who I think he is, we'll be quite safe.'

But *was* this Resaldar the son of Jack Haverington, Bella asked herself. For all they knew, the name might be as common in Afghanistan as Jack was in England. The Resaldar she had been expecting to find—the timid, cowed young boy of her imagining—might be long dead, and this haughty princeling a completely different Resaldar.

But, a doubtful voice in her mind protested, *a totally unconnected Afghan named Resaldar, who just happened to possess the European colouring of blue eyes and tawny hair, and who spoke English perfectly?*

It was hardly likely.

The truth came to her quite suddenly. She didn't *want* this Resaldar to be their cousin. The thought of him lording it at Haverington Hall was quite galling.

Then, with relief, she remembered something else. Resaldar himself could never inherit Haverington Hall, for he was illegitimate. Only Jack Haverington could inherit, if he was still alive. Mr Munday, the lawyer, had explained it all carefully to her before she left England.

Her thoughts were interrupted by Resaldar himself. 'Now,' he said, studying the party of captives, 'pray tell me what is the reason for your curiosity about Shapoora and, by definition, myself.'

Lionel Bromley too had sensed a need for caution, and it was clear that he shared Bella's reservations. He gave the others a warning look, indicating that they should leave the talking to him.

'Before we explain,' he answered Resaldar, 'we must be certain that you are who you claim to be. The Resaldar we came to seek was a prisoner of the Infidels, a slave. We would also need to know who your parents are, and if possible to speak to them—'

'Indeed?' There was something inexplicably menacing about Resaldar as he stood regarding Bromley, his arms folded across his chest. But his voice was mild enough as he continued—'My parents are, regrettably, dead. My father was English, and my mother was Shazeen, the daughter of the Emir. I am, therefore, the Emir's grandson.'

His voice changed suddenly, and flayed their ears like a whiplash. 'And out of respect for the dynastic blood which flows in my veins you will call me Highness when you speak to me, and salaam before addressing me!'

There was a moment's tense silence. Why, Bella wondered, had the Reverend Percy Dawkes contented himself with only that one letter written to Great-Uncle Howard? But perhaps he *had* written again, and the old man had simply destroyed the letters.

There was something so compelling in Resaldar's gaze that Lionel Bromley placed his right palm on his forehead and bowed low. 'It would seem, Highness, that you are indeed the Resaldar we came to seek—'

He was interrupted by the unheralded arrival in the room of a man dressed in western clothes. He glanced at them and grinned.

'Heigh-ho, me maties!' he greeted them in an unmistakable Irish brogue. Then he turned to Resaldar and salaamed, and began addressing him in an unknown tongue.

Bella studied the man, trying to slot him into place in

this unlikely setting. Resaldar had clearly been expecting him and had probably sent for him. He was in his early thirties, perhaps, tall and lithe, with russet hair and intelligent, watchful hazel eyes. His manner towards Resaldar seemed to be a subtle blend of deference and familiarity. What was an Irishman doing in Shapoora? Then she dismissed him from her mind, for she had other matters on which to concentrate.

Under cover of Resaldar's conversation with the Irishman, she whispered to Lionel Bromley and Simon, 'Don't disclose who we are. Invent some other reason for our interest in Shapoora.'

'But why?' Simon mouthed.

'I'll explain later.'

'The tribe lives by kidnapping travellers along the Khyber Pass,' the missionary had written to Great-Uncle Howard. Obviously, Bella thought grimly, Jack Haverington's son was keeping up the tribal traditions. If he knew that Simon now stood to inherit the estate— an estate which Resaldar no doubt considered should morally be his—he would not hesitate to demand a ransom for their release which would milk Simon's inheritance of every penny.

As it was, he would probably demand a collective ransom for them from the British authorities.

We'll make up some story to account for our interest in him, Bella thought, *and when we have been freed, Simon and I will return to England and forget that we have a cousin named Resaldar in Afghanistan . . .*

Resaldar's conversation with the Irishman had come to an end. He regarded them with a grim smile.

'At my request,' he said, 'my friend Flynn has been examining your baggage which was seized by my guards. I know, now, why you have been seeking me.'

'Oh . . .' Bella murmured in dismay.

Resaldar ignored her, and fixed his gaze on Lionel Bromley. 'You are a correspondent for a British newspaper. I don't know why you chose to travel with two boys and a young woman, but your interest in me is now clear. You have been asking questions about me and my village, because you have heard how my parents and I were captured by the Infidels and treated like slaves while they held us to ransom. You thought it would make a titiliating story for your newspaper, did you not, to write about the half-English slave who contrived to become the Khan of Shapoora!'

'Well—' Lionel began.

'I care nothing for England,' Resaldar continued coldly, 'and I am indifferent to the possibility of becoming a five days' wonder there. But British news inevitably finds its way to Afghanistan too, and it does not suit me to have attention drawn to me in this way. I cannot, therefore, allow you to go free and write your sensational report.'

'I'll give an undertaking to write nothing, if that is what you wish,' Bromley said.

'I'm afraid your undertaking will not be enough.' Resaldar favoured him with an inscrutable look. 'Besides,' he confirmed Bella's suspicions, 'I have other reasons for keeping you prisoner; reasons why you were captured in the first place.'

Nicolette Prewitt suddenly gave vent to the hysteria which had been simmering inside her. 'I have nothing to do with the others!' she shrilled. 'You must let *me* go! You'll be sorry if you don't! My father is an important man, a general with the British Army, and he—'

'Is he, now?' It was the Irishman who interrupted her, a look of mingled admiration and speculation in his eyes as he studied her.

Resaldar, too, was regarding Nicolette with interest.

'A general . . . How very fortuitous. What is his name?'

'Prewitt. General Clive Prewitt, and he is also a personal friend of both General Maude and Major Cavagnari! So if you know what is good for you, you'll conduct me safely to Jellalabad!'

Resaldar and the Irishman, Flynn, exchanged glances. Then Resaldar said mildly, 'I am afraid, Miss Prewitt, that I cannot let you go.' He showed his teeth in a sardonic smile. 'Notwithstanding your important connections. You will now be taken to join the harem''

'No!' Nicolette screamed. 'You unspeakable brute—I won't be part of your filthy harem!'

'Jasus bless your innocence, darlin',' Flynn interposed, 'but His Highness is not after making you his concubine! Harem is simply the word for the women's quarters.'

An austere, distant look entered Resaldar's eyes as he realised what Nicolette had been thinking. 'I am not a barbarian, Miss Prewitt,' he said quietly. 'I am not even a Muslim, reserving for himself the privilege of a personal harem. But for reasons which don't concern you I have persuaded the Infidels to adopt the Muslim faith, and like most converts they are zealous in their religious observance. You will therefore be confined to the harem, and you will wear the *chador* and veil—'

''Tis a holy shame that such loveliness should be hidden,' Flynn mused regretfully.

Resaldar ignored him. 'You will help the women with their everyday domestic tasks, Miss Prewitt, and you will not be allowed contact with the male prisoners.'

Nicolette caught her breath. 'Domestic tasks—that's almost as outrageous—'

Resaldar interrupted her by clapping his hands once more, and the two guards reappeared. At a word from him each took Nicolette firmly by an arm and began to bear her, struggling and screaming, from the room.

For the first time since she had met Nicolette, Bella felt sorry for her, and dismayed by her fate—a fate which she herself would have had to share if her femininity had been known. Until now, no one had questioned her sex; even Nicolette, largely uninterested in everything but her own affairs, had accepted that Bella was a youth named Stanley. And obviously, whoever had searched their belongings had assumed that the female garments belonged to Nicolette.

It was unfortunate that she had disclosed her father's rank and importance, for it would only serve to increase the ransom which Resaldar meant to demand for them, and so inevitably lengthen the term of their captivity.

Resaldar began to speak again, and it suddenly became clear to Bella that there might be a more humiliating and undignified fate in store for her than mere banishment to the harem.

'Take the three prisoners away, Flynn,' Resaldar was saying. 'See that they are adequately housed. It won't be necessary to confine them, but to discourage any notion they may have of escaping, take away their breeches and their shoes.'

Colour flamed in Bella's face as she realised the implications of his command. She turned upon Resaldar, too angry and outraged for caution.

'And you claim that you're not a barbarian! You're far worse! Do you imagine it's *civilised* to trade in human beings? You're no better than the Infidels who kidnapped your parents and held them to ransom!'

He regarded her with one eyebrow raised. 'And you are a remarkably foolhardy and reckless youth to address me in such a manner—'

'Oh, stop trying to frighten me! I'm not impressed by your position as Khan of this tin-pot kingdom! And you needn't think,' she added furiously, 'that I'd call you Highness either, or ever demean myself by salaaming to you!'

A look of mingled amusement and interest entered his eyes. 'I could very easily force you to do both, you know,' he murmured. 'Tell me—what is your name, boy?'

In spite of her anger, Bella had the wit to adhere to the name by which Bromley had introduced her to Nicolette. 'Stanley. And if your Irish friend attempts to relieve me of my breeches, he'll be extremely sorry!'

Resaldar's lips twitched. 'In that case,' he said suavely, 'I must not ask him to put himself at risk on my behalf. I shall relieve you of your breeches myself.'

As he advanced towards her, Bella forgot all her earlier resolutions and her caution. 'Great-Uncle Howard would have been extremely proud of you!' she cried bitingly. 'What a shame it is that he never met the grandson who matches him so well in sheer odium and loathsomeness!'

Resaldar had stopped in his tracks. 'My *grandfather*?'

'My brother Simon and I are your second cousins,' Bella said flatly. 'We travelled to this benighted country because, heaven help us, we had foolish ideas about rescuing you from the Infidels! And Mr Bromley was helping us to find you.'

Resaldar's expression had grown totally blank. 'Why did you not speak of this before?' he demanded.

Bella hesitated. She could only hope, now, that he would not realise Simon stood to inherit Great-Uncle Howard's estate.

'Once I had met you,' she said at last, 'it was not a relationship I wished to claim.'

'So!' Resaldar's voice had turned stark and bitter. 'Let me assure you, Cousin Stanley, that it's not a relationship which gives *me* any pride or pleasure either! For twenty years I witnessed my father waiting to be rescued by my English relatives. For twenty years I watched the hope in him shrivel and finally die as he came to realise they did not mean to lift a finger to help any of us! So do not expect me to be grateful to you and your brother for this belated gesture!'

'We did not know—' Bella began.

'Someone must have known! My father sent news of our fate through one of the kidnap-victims released by the Infidels. He sent it to someone who could be relied upon to write to England. And the letter must have reached its destination, or you would not be here now! You are much too late, dear Cousin! My father died, a slave, and my mother did not survive him for long. As for me, I require no help from anyone. I control my own destiny!'

Bella was silent, appalled at the thought of the slow torture which Jack Haverington must have endured as he waited in vain for a response to his appeal for help. She could not really blame Resaldar for his bitterness.

He broke the silence, his voice flat now. 'You are still my prisoners, cousins or not. However, you are entitled to be treated with civility and with the hospitality due to family connections. Please go with Flynn. He will see you comfortably housed, and ensure that you have everything you require.'

The Irishman had moved to the door. As they were about to follow him out, Resaldar said suddenly 'Cousin Stanley, you will oblige me by joining me for tiffin. A servant will be sent to fetch you.'

Curious, and a little apprehensive about sharing a meal with Resaldar, Bella followed Flynn outside. Now she had the opportunity of studying the village more closely.

Many of the houses had been built in the domed *yurt* shape, a style borrowed from the tents of the Mongols. The whole village was enclosed in blank mud walls, with bastions and high watch-towers with loopholes through which to repel any raids by rival freebooters. Several of the houses were surrounded by fruit trees, with a threshing floor close at hand, where black-robed women were at work.

Lionel Bromley was studying Flynn thoughtfully as the latter led the way to one of the domed houses. 'I've heard of you,' Bromley said abruptly. 'You're Seamus Flynn, some-time purveyor of commodities to the British troops, for which you charge extortionate prices—'

'Indeed, a man has to live,' Flynn said cheerfully. 'Here we are, me lads. Settle yerselves in.'

The house was principally furnished with wooden charpoys, cushions and rugs. There were, Bella was relieved to find, three or four partitions which could be used as separate sleeping chambers. As if by magic, servants appeared with their luggage and withdrew again. Silent women, heavily veiled and robed in the black *chador* which covered them from chin to toes, glided into the rooms, bearing bowls of water for washing. Bella looked at them, and spared a sympathetic thought for Nicolette, entombed in the harem, forced to wear robes and veil and busy herself with lowly tasks. It also made her more determined than ever not to share Nicolette's fate.

When she was certain that all the servants had withdrawn from the house, Bella washed and changed into clean breeches and shirt. Then, with her hair falling to her shoulders, she went in search of Lionel Bromley.

He had just finished shaving. He put his razor down, and looked at her with a frown. 'I've remembered something else about Flynn,' he announced. 'He was said to be involved in running guns to Afghan tribesmen. The man is an opportunist, completely without morals or scruples. I wonder what he is doing here, installed at Shapoora . . .'

'No doubt he and my cousin have a great deal in common,' Bella said scathingly. 'Mr Bromley, I apologise for having been the cause of landing you in this mess. Frankly, I wish I had remained in blissful ignorance of Resaldar's very existence!'

He took her hands in a warm grasp. 'I am the one who should be apologising. If I had been more discreet in my enquiries about Shapoora—' He broke off, frowning. 'There was something about the reaction of the Khans when I mentioned Shapoora—It was almost as if they had a superstitious dread of the villagers, or of their leader . . .'

Bella sighed, and changed the subject. 'I came to ask your help, Mr Bromley, because Simon does not yet possess a razor. Will you please use yours to cut off my hair?'

'What—all of it?'

'As much as is necessary,' Bella said firmly. 'I cannot hope to go on hiding it underneath a sun helmet, and I have absolutely no intention of being banished to the harem, and forced to retire behind the *chador* and veil.'

'No. Poor Nicolette.' Lionel Bromley grinned. 'Perhaps it will prove to be a chastening experience for her. Very well, Miss Stanley. I'll do my best.'

Bella stood patiently while Bromley hacked at her hair with the razor. It was as well, she thought with resignation, that she had no inflated opinion of her own looks, so that the loss of her hair would not cause her much heartache.

'How do I look?' she demanded, when Bromley

stepped back to inspect his handiwork.

'Quite enchanting,' he said softly.

Bella flushed under his gaze. 'I don't wish to look enchanting,' she protested. 'I want to look like a boy!' She raised her hands to her head, and cried with dismay—'It *curls*!'

'Indeed it does, in a most beguiling way.'

To Bella's relief, Simon interrupted them at that moment. She was not accustomed to open admiration in the gaze of a man, and it disconcerted her. Simon's eyes widened at sight of her.

'You don't look a day older than sixteen, Bella!' he exclaimed, and added with disgust, 'It isn't fair! Cousin Resaldar thinks you're a boy, and as a boy you look younger than I, so why did he invite *you* to eat with him instead of me?'

'If you imagine that I *want* to eat with him—' Bella began, reaching for the looking-glass which Lionel Bromley was holding out to her. She stopped, and studied her reflection.

Who would ever have imagined that her hair, free from its confining snood and cut short, would cover her head in bubbly, frivolous curls more auburn than brown? It was quite true that the curls, together with her smooth fair skin, made her look absurdly young and vulnerable. And, she conceded, too pretty by half for a boy. But while Resaldar would no doubt consider her something of a milksop, there was no reason why he should leap to the conclusion that she was a female.

'Well, *I* should like to be alone in his company,' Simon was saying broodingly. 'There are a hundred and one questions I should like to ask him. My goodness, he must be extremely brave to have forced the Infidels to make him their chief . . .'

Her young brother, Bella thought sourly, had swiftly

fallen under Resaldar's spell, and was already beginning to hero-worship him. She felt in no danger of emulating him as she set out, shortly afterwards, in the wake of the servant who had come to summon her to Resaldar's presence.

This time she was taken into a different room in the house. The walls were hung with silk, and quite exquisite carpets covered the floors. Resaldar was already seated by a low, carved table. He stared at her intently when she entered.

'You're even younger than I thought,' he said abruptly. 'I really don't know why I sought the company of a child. Perhaps your nerve and your impudence amuses me. Sit down, Cousin Stanley.'

A servant padded in softly and placed beautifully arranged bouquets of flowers at each end of the table. Another arrived with a metal water-jug from which he filled a bowl in which Bella discovered she was meant to dip her fingers during the meal.

A great bustle on the stairs outside preceded the arrival of the food. A cloth was laid across the table, and two *chapattis*, or large flat cakes of unleavened bread, were placed before them. One of these, Bella found, was meant to serve as a plate. Then the cooks arrived with pieces of fowl, kid and mutton frizzling on large spits. The meats were accompanied by various pilaus and condiments, all quite delicious.

Bella looked up, to find Resaldar leaning back in his seat and studying her with a frowning gaze. But all he said was, 'Try some of this, Cousin. It's snow water.'

'Snow?' she echoed, taking the silver drinking cup from him. 'In this heat?'

He smiled. 'It is collected in winter by the women, and stored in pits lined with chaff. In summer it is cut out as required.' The smile left his face, and he changed the subject abruptly. 'Tell me about my grandfather. You said he was loathsome.'

'Yes, I'm afraid he was. You also have him to thank for the fact that you and your parents were never rescued. He put the letter informing him of your fate away in a secret drawer, and told no one of its existence. It was only found recently, after his death.'

Resaldar drummed his fingers upon the table. 'Poor father . . . I loved him, but he was not a man of great courage. He relied utterly on help from outside. For myself, I realised when I was quite young that I would have to help myself.'

'How *did* you become Khan of Shapoora?' Bella asked curiously.

'By using my wits and my personality. By proving, from an early age, that I was more intelligent, more resourceful, more courageous than anyone else.' He spoke with a total lack of humility. 'Slowly, by degrees, I forced my will upon the Infidels. When we faced attack by another tribe I made them see that I was the only one who could save them from annihilation. My price was the title and position of Khan.'

He smiled derisively. 'Some of the other tribes believe I used witchcraft to raise myself to the status of Khan. It's a belief which I encourage, for reasons of my own.'

So that, Bella thought, was the reason for the superstitious awe which Bromley had encountered when he enquired about Shapoora . . .

'As for the Infidels,' Resaldar went on, 'they have not regretted our pact. Life for them has become easier since I took control. For example, they were, by tradition, a tribe of nomads. They had been driven out of the Hindu Kush, and they wandered through the Sulaiman Mountains, only using Shapoora as an occasional makeshift base. I made them see how much more prosperous they would be, living a settled existence.'

'And you persuaded them to adopt the Muslim faith, so that they can no longer truthfully be called Infidels.' Bella frowned. 'But you yourself, did not adopt it, you said. Why not?'

'What an inquisitive child you are,' Resaldar murmured. 'I wonder why I tolerate all these personal questions. No doubt I shall eventually be forced to turn Muslim, for the sake of expediency, but I was christened soon after my birth.'

'You were *christened*—' Bella said sharply. 'How did that come about?'

He raised his eyebrows at her, and answered with exaggerated patience. 'Nothing will serve, it seems, but that you should learn every detail of my life. You will already know, from the information which my father succeeded in smuggling out of Shapoora, that he and my mother were forced to flee when she found that she was expecting a child.'

'Yes—yes.'

'They took shelter in a Buddhist cave to await my birth. They lived on what my father could forage or hunt for, and sometimes they were given food by nomads or other travellers.'

'One of those travellers was the Anglican missionary who wrote to Great-Uncle Howard,' Bella put in thoughtfully.

'That is correct. Bad weather conditions forced him to share my parents' shelter for several months. He took the opportunity of joining them in marriage, and he was still there when I was born, some months later. Although the weather had improved, he stayed on for a while longer so that he could christen me.'

An exclamation of dismay from Bella interrupted him. He gave her a sardonic smile. 'It displeases you that

I am less of a barbarian than you thought me, Cousin?'

'No.' Her voice was toneless. 'If your parents were married before you were born, then—' She swallowed. 'You are the legitimate heir to Haverington Hall, and not my brother Simon. You won't have to live by kidnap and plunder any longer, Resaldar. You may go to England and take possession of your grandfather's estates. I'm sure that must please you mightily.'

'*Please* me?' There was something reckless and mocking in his voice. 'A tin-pot inheritance in England? Oh no, thank you, Cousin Stanley!'

She flushed, recognising the taunting echo of her own adjective to describe Shapoora. 'I assure you,' she said stiffly, 'Haverington Hall is part of a large and prosperous estate, comprising several farms—'

'I have my sights set on something rather more illustrious,' Resaldar interrupted. His blue eyes were very vivid and alive as they rested on her. 'I intend to seize the throne of Afghanistan, Cousin Stanley.'

Bella stared back at him, suspecting an elaborate joke. But his expression brought it slowly home to her that he was in deadly earnest.

'I think,' she said, her voice flat, 'that your success in grabbing the chieftaincy of Shapoora must have gone to your head. You're stark, raving mad—'

He rose and moved towards her, pulling her without gentleness to her feet. She was uncomfortably conscious of him as he towered over her, his hands fastened about her wrists.

'Don't try my tolerance too far, Cousin Stanley,' he said softly, ominously. 'You may be an amusing young cub, but you would do well to remember than you are in my power. And you are, without a doubt, addressing the future Emir of Kabul. Remember that, too!'

Her heart was beating disquietingly fast. It was, she

told herself, because even the most casual physical contact between them increased the danger that he might discover her true sex.

She tried to speak calmly. 'Because I am in your power, as you so rightly pointed out, I'll withdraw my remark. And if you will let me go, and explain to me how you mean to seize the throne, I'll try to feign the respect you demand.'

He gave a sudden crack of amused laughter, and dropped her wrists. Then he studied her with a puzzled air. 'You must be younger than Simon, for you said that *he* was to have inherited the English estate. And yet— and yet . . . There is something astonishingly composed and mature about you, Cousin Stanley—'

'I was always the dull, bookish one of the family,' Bella said colourlessly. 'No doubt that will explain it. But we were talking about you, Cousin Resaldar. How could you possibly seize the throne of Afghanistan? I imagine that your grandfather, the Emir of Kabul, would be well able to resist an attempted coup by the tribesmen of Shapoora!'

Resaldar had resumed his seat, and with a feeling of relief Bella sat down too. 'My grandfather is dead,' he said without emotion. 'My good friend Flynn keeps me up to date with all the news from Kabul. It seems that the Emir had gone to Russia to try and enlist help against the British invasion, and while there he contracted some illness and died suddenly. That means that the throne is vacant at a time when the country is racked by war.'

'And you, as the Emir's grandson, are the only claimant to the throne?'

'By no means,' Resaldar returned in a calm voice. 'My grandfather is survived by several sons, and numerous grandsons, brothers and nephews—all of them scrambling for the throne.'

'And you feel *your* claim will succeed.' Bella shook her head. 'I don't know much about such matters, but I would have thought one needed a strong army in order to seize a throne against such overwhelming opposition. And you have only the tribesmen of Shapoora to back you—'

Resaldar gave her a brilliant smile of pure triumph. 'As you say, Cousin Stanley, one needs a strong army. And I have such an army. The army of Her Imperial Majesty Queen Victoria, no less!'

'The British Army?' Bella echoed. 'Do you honestly imagine they will help you? Why should they?'

Resaldar did not answer directly. 'Tell me,' he said instead. 'Why do you suppose you are being held prisoner here?'

Bella did not try to hide her contempt. 'Because you mean to exact a ransom for us, of course.'

He was impervious to the scorn in her voice. 'Ah yes, but what a ransom! It was surely fate which sent you blundering through the Khyber Pass, asking questions about Shapoora, just when I needed British prisoners. And only a kindly fate could have arranged that Miss Nicolette Prewitt should be travelling with you!'

His smile broadened. 'I hardly think that her high-ranking, fond father and his good friends General Maude and Major Cavagnari would wish to take the slightest risk with her safety!'

'I see . . .' Bella said slowly. 'Yes, I see—'

'I rather thought you would, Cousin Stanley, an intelligent youth like you.' Resaldar's voice was smooth. 'You are my hostages. To ensure your safe return—and particularly the safe return of Miss Prewitt—the British Army will be forced to help me grab the throne of Afghanistan!'

CHAPTER
THREE

INSIDE THE domed house which was to serve as their prison, Bella was recounting Resaldar's ambitious, grandiose plans to her brother and Lionel Bromley. She had been abruptly dismissed by Resaldar, as if he had grown bored with her company, and she was still smarting with indignation as she recalled the imperious manner in which he had clapped his hands for his servants, and had her summarily escorted from his presence even while she was trying to point out to him how unworkable his crazy schemes were.

Now she voiced her arguments to Lionel and Simon. 'The British Army will refuse to be blackmailed!'

'Of course they will,' Lionel agreed. 'As soon as they learn that we are being held here, they'll mount a surprise raid on Shapoora. We must be prepared for that eventuality, so that we may co-operate fully with our rescuers.' He added, frowning, 'A way must be found to warn Miss Prewitt. She knows nothing of what is afoot.'

'I'll try to think of something,' Bella said. She went on vengefully, 'I don't give much for Resaldar's chances when the Army get their hands on him!'

At that moment the air was rent by the sound of a *muezzin* calling the Muslim faithful to prayer. Bella moved to the doorway, and stared outside. Tribesmen were prostrating themselves in the dust, their faces turned towards Mecca. The dying rays of the sun caught and reflected a flash of light from the direction of one of the loopholes in the Khan's dwelling, and Bella realised that it was the single jewel in Resaldar's head-dress reflecting in the sun.

She gazed at him for a moment, transfixed. He was unaware of her scrutiny. His head was thrown back, his vivid blue eyes proud, arrogant and utterly sure of his own power and authority as he surveyed his subjects kneeling in the faith to which he had converted them.

Bella found Simon by her side, his gaze also caught by Resaldar. 'They won't—' her brother began uneasily. 'The Army won't *execute* Cousin Resaldar, will they, Bella?'

It was Lionel who answered for her. 'I daresay they will do just that. After all, he is threatening to execute *us* unless the Army help him.'

Bella stirred restlessly. 'That is sheer bluff, I'm sure. Resaldar wouldn't—'

'It would be a mistake to underrate your cousin's ruthlessness, Miss Stanley,' Lionel said quietly. He gestured towards the prostrate tribesmen. 'The Afghans are a stubborn, brave, vindictive and cruel people. They have to be, for the weaklings among them die young, unable to cope with the struggle. From the moment of their birth they face an unceasing battle for survival in this pitiless country. And these particular tribesmen of Shapoora—erstwhile Infidels from Kafiristan in the Hindu Kush—were used to roam wild and free, marauding and plundering, bowing their knee to no one—'

'Until Resaldar subdued them!' Simon put in breathlessly, caught up in admiration for their cousin.

'Precisely,' Lionel agreed. 'Do you think such a man would flinch from executing a handful of hostages? He would *have* to execute us, unless the Army kill him first, for otherwise he would lose his credibility and authority with the tribesmen.'

Before either Bella or Simon could respond, their attention was caught by a furtive black-clad figure slipping through the archway of the harem. As soon as she had gained the outer wall she threw both furtiveness and caution to the wind. Lifting her black *chador* in one hand, her veil and golden tresses flying in the breeze, Nicolette Prewitt presented a dramatic, fleeing figure silhouetted against the burnt umber of the surrounding hills. Neither the praying tribesmen nor the women in the harem had noticed her escape.

'The idiot!' Bella said breathlessly. 'Where does she imagine she is running to? I'd best go after her—'

Skirting the perimeter of the praying tribesman, Bella set off in pursuit. Then she became aware that Flynn, the Irishman, had also witnessed Nicolette's flight and had set out from the Khan's dwelling to head her off. He caught her in his arms and held her while she wept hysterically.

Bella slackened her pace, and moved as unobtrusively as she could towards them. There might just be an opportunity to warn Nicolette that she should be on the alert for a surprise attack by the British Army.

Flynn was stroking Nicolette's golden hair when Bella approached unseen, keeping in the shadows. 'Whisht, *acushla*,' he murmured. 'Cryin' will only redden your beautiful eyes.'

'Please—*please*—' Nicolette sobbed. 'My father is extremely wealthy—he will pay anything—if only you'd help me to get out of this place—'

There was a reflective look in Flynn's eyes as he gazed down at her. 'Will he, now . . . ?'

Was it possible, Bella wondered, that Flynn might be persuaded, with the promise of money, to change sides? Then she remembered what his rewards would be if

Resaldar should succeed in claiming the throne of Afghanistan.

No, Flynn the opportunist would try to extort money from General Prewitt if the chance was there, but he would also continue to help Resaldar with his schemes.

'Only be patient, me lovely,' the Irishman was soothing Nicolette. 'You'll be leavin' Shapoora before long, and you'll have Seamus Flynn to thank. Trust me.'

'You'll help me?' Nicolette appealed pathetically.

'I don't see,' Bella interrupted, stepping from the shadows, 'how he could possibly help you, Miss Prewitt, since he is helping my Cousin Resaldar, and you are their most important hostage. They hope to force your father, and through him the British Army, to place my cousin on the throne of Afghanistan. Of course, it's ludicrous to imagine that the Army would be blackmailed.'

Would Nicolette understand that the Army was much more likely to respond by raiding Shapoora in an attempt to free the hostages? It was impossible to tell, for she had begun to weep again in earnest.

Flynn looked at Bella with dislike. 'You're a mite too big for your breeches, me boy! What d'you think yer doin' here?'

'Why,' Bella said calmly, 'I imagine I'm nipping in the bud your newly hatched scheme to extract money from Miss Prewitt's father by pretending that you'll be responsible for her release!'

Flynn's face darkened. He released Nicolette, and took a step towards Bella. ''Tis time ye were taught a little respect for your elders—'

'If you lay one finger on me,' Bella said clearly, 'I shall tell my cousin. You may have noticed that I'm quite a favourite with him.'

Flynn stopped in his tracks. His anger gave way to a

look of speculation. 'Yes, so it would seem. Though why himself should be so taken with a young spalpeen like yerself—' He shrugged and smiled, a smile of easy charm, intended to rob his words of any sting. Then he turned away, taking Nicolette's arm. 'Come, me darlin'. I fear 'tis back to the harem with you for now.'

Bella returned thoughtfully to the domed house. She had, she thought, taken Flynn's measure. In the same way as he could not resist the stray chance of making money from Nicolette's father, he was equally alive to the necessity of keeping on the right side of anyone Resaldar favoured. He could not help responding to whatever opportunity arose to further his own interests.

And yet Resaldar appeared to be unaware of this trait in the Irishman. For all the ingenuity and ruthlessness with which he had clawed his way from slave to chieftain, for all the education received from his English father, Resaldar did not recognise this kind of sophisticated western duplicity. He lived in a world in which one's friends and enemies were clear-cut and readily identifiable, with no grey areas in between.

Bella's thoughts turned to Nicolette. Despite her unlikable ways, the girl was to be pitied. She had clearly been cosseted and spoilt all her life, with the result that she had no inner resources on which to fall back. Because of this she was finding their present circumstances doubly unendurable, and her sheltered upbringing also made her unable to see through Flynn.

The tribesmen had finished their devotions, and Bella saw that they were now engaged in building a huge bonfire in the open space beyond the village houses. Soon its rays were illuminating the dusk fitfully, casting mysterious shadows in places, sharply high-lighting others. The effect of firelight and shadow on sun-baked walls and high watch-towers was somehow pagan, wholly foreign and not a little frightening.

'I wish,' Bella said forcefully to Lionel and her brother. 'I wish I had never conceived the notion of coming to Afghanistan to look for my wretched Cousin Resaldar and his parents!'

'*I* don't,' Lionel returned softly. 'I should not otherwise have met you.'

She felt a flush suffusing her face. She had no coquettish ways with which to parry the admiration shown by a man, and she was totally unaware that her very confusion, her heightened colour and her tremulous mouth lent her an air of vulnerability which went straight to the heart.

She was not aware, either, that Resaldar had approached, accompanied by an entourage, and that he was regarding her from the shadows. He stepped forward into the light, wearing a frowning, puzzled expression. But all he said was,

'My men are to give a display of tribal dancing. You are all required to join us by the fire.'

As they followed him and his attendants, Bella noticed sourly that his progress had taken on a regal pace. His subjects bowed low in his path, or caught hold of his hand to kiss it.

Bella could not deny that there was a kind of savage splendour to the dancing which began as soon as Resaldar had given the signal for it. To the accompaniment of drummers and pipers, the tribesmen began to gyrate around the fire.

Seizing an undrawn sword by the scabbard, each dancer drew the sword, circled it around his head and then steadied it by resting the blade on his head and sheathing it again. It was all done in one seemingly fluid movement, while the firelight flashed on the steel of the swords and the music throbbed and wailed in perfect time to the motion.

When the dancing came to an end, Simon's eyes were bright with excitement. 'Poor Miss Prewitt,' he breathed. 'Having to miss that!'

'Yes.' Bella turned to Resaldar. 'Cousin, is it quite necessary for her to be kept in—what is the word— *purdah*? She has nothing in common with the other women—she cannot even speak their tongue . . .'

'It is quite necessary,' he interrupted. 'No exception can be made for her. Besides, she could if she wished converse with Fawzia, who speaks English perfectly.'

'Fawzia? Who is she?'

Resaldar did not respond immediately, and when he did his tone was discouraging. 'She is a princess of the Hazara tribe.'

And what is she doing at Shapoora? Bella wondered, but after a look at her cousin's forbidding face decided not to form the question.

Lionel, who had obviously also been reasoning that it would be to their advantage if all the hostages could be contained together, addressed Resaldar. 'Your Highness, since Miss Prewitt is not a Muslim, surely your people will accept it if she is allowed to live outside the harem?'

'They will not,' Resaldar replied shortly.

'But they accept *you* as their Khan,' Bella persisted, 'and you are not a Muslim—'

'Don't,' Resaldar warned irritably, 'test my patience too far, Cousin Stanley, or you may well find yourself confined to the harem too!'

Bella's heart began to beat uncomfortably fast. 'Why on earth should *I*—?' she began.

'The harem is not only for women, but for children too. And you are scarcely more than a child, are you?'

Simon decided to risk a question, perhaps to divert

attention from Bella. 'Why did you persuade the tribesmen to adopt the Muslim faith, Cousin Resaldar?'

'Because I reasoned that they would be more easily
controlled if they accepted the discipline of a religious
doctrine. A Mullah who had been captured in the Pass
was persuaded to instruct them in the teachings of the
Koran.'

'But you declined to become a Muslim?' Lionel
ventured. 'Would that not be a handicap if you were to
become Emir of Kabul—?'

'*When* I become Emir of Kabul,' Resaldar interrupted, 'I hope to bring religious tolerance to my reign.' His
tone hardened. 'And now that we are on that subject, let
us discuss how my demands are to be brought before the
British Army. I have decided to send one of the hostages
as an emissary.'

There was a moment's silence. Then Lionel Bromley
spoke. 'Why not your friend Seamus Flynn?'

It was the Irishman himself who answered the question with a grin. 'I think you know why. The small matter
of supplyin' guns to Afghan tribesmen . . .'

Resaldar nodded. 'The Army may be tempted to put
him against a wall and shoot him.'

'In that case, I am the obvious choice,' Lionel
suggested.

'I think not. You may decide not to return, but to
write your sensational newspaper story from a safe
distance instead. My Cousin Stanley, however,'
Resaldar went on, 'would certainly not fail to return,
and so abandon his brother to his fate.'

'You mean to send Be—' Lionel began, and hastily
caught himself. 'Your Highness—a young boy—'

'If one of us has to go, it should be I!' Simon interrupted eagerly.

'No. You do not have your brother's maturity, his

self-possession. It comes, I understand, from his being the bookish one of the family.' Resaldar quoted Bella's explanation with a thoughtful, puzzled shake of his head.

'I cannot allow you to send—' Lionel began obstinately. In another moment, instinct told Bella, he would reveal the truth about her sex.

She shook her head slightly at him in warning, and said, 'Of course I am prepared to be your messenger, Cousin Resaldar. I welcome the chance of being able to bring back to you the Army's scornful rejection of your outrageous plans!'

Resaldar's smile was bland. 'I knew I could count on you, Cousin. You will leave in the morning, accompanied by armed guides, for the Army camp at Gandamak, and deliver a note to the Viceroy's Plenipotentiary, Major Cavagnari.'

He rose. 'Now, I would suggest that you retire for the night.'

'It isn't fair!' Simon uttered his familiar lament as the three hostages returned to the domed house. '*I* should have been the one chosen to go! I should have liked to show Cousin Resaldar that he is not the only brave, resourceful one in the family . . .'

Lionel said nothing, but later he came to speak to Bella alone in the partition which she had chosen as her own sleeping quarters.

'Miss Stanley, the very idea of your travelling alone through these mountains with a band of ruffianly tribesmen is madness! Your cousin must be told the truth— that he cannot send you—'

Bella laid a hand on his arm. 'Mr Bromley, if I didn't go, then who would Resaldar send in my place? There is only Simon. And my blood runs cold at the very thought of my reckless, impetuous brother being trusted with the mission. You heard what he said: he would leap at any chance of attempting some daring-do to impress Resaldar.'

She smiled. 'I shall be quite safe. The ruffianly tribesmen will be there to protect me, and not to harm me. And when I return it will be with some plan of campaign drawn up by the Army for our rescue and release.'

Lionel lifted his hand, and covered hers where it lay on his arm. 'You are so brave!' he muttered. 'Bella—may I call you that?—I know we have not been acquainted for long, but your courage, your spirit . . .' He stopped, and smiled. 'I believe you know what I am trying to say.'

'I—' Bella faltered, her colour rising.

'No, do not answer me now. This war in Afghanistan cannot last much longer; when it is over I shall apply for a post as a home correspondent in England. I have some money saved. I can offer you security and comfort, Bella, a lifetime of tranquillity to make up for the present danger and discomfort facing us.'

He lifted her hand and brought it to his lips. 'Think it over, my dear. I shall not speak of it again until we are out of this present peril. And now I shall say good night. My thoughts will be with you on your journey tomorrow.'

He left her, and she prepared for bed, her mind in a turmoil. Lionel was a good man, a kind, concerned man. He was more than she had any right to expect at her age, and with her lack of fortune or beauty. Moreover, she had long ago given up hope of receiving a proposal of marriage from anyone. So what was the matter with her that she felt so strangely depressed?

It was, she realised with a sudden flash of intuition, because he had offered her tranquillity when she craved excitement. He had offered her security and comfort when what she had wanted was passion. And he had kissed her hand when she had hoped for—

She stifled the thought, and told herself—*You're mad, Bella Stanley. Be grateful that you are to be rescued from a life of lonely spinsterhood, and make up your mind to accept Lionel Bromley.*

In the morning they met only briefly before Bella set out with an armed escort of tribesmen for the British camp. There was no time for any private conversation, but Bella looked at Lionel's pleasant, craggy face and tried to imprint it on her memory. She *would* marry him when all this was over . . .

Resaldar arrived in person to hand over the note which Bella was to deliver to Major Cavagnari. With his tawny-gold hair showing beneath the head-dress, his intensely blue eyes and his height as he towered over her, he looked more like a conquering Viking than a Pretender to the throne of Afghanistan.

He helped Bella to mount one of the spirited Waziri horses which had been saddled. He seemed to be forcibly struck by the contrast between her small, slight and defenceless form and those of her escort, looking murderous armed with long Khyber knives, spears and flint-locks. Resaldar caught his lower lip between his teeth, and said abruptly,

'I would have sent someone else if it had been possible . . .'

Softness from him was both unexpected and unwelcome. Bella wanted nothing to dilute her dislike of him. She said tartly, 'And denied me the pleasure of dashing all your grand hopes? Oh no, Cousin Resaldar!'

The softness vanished; he nodded curtly and turned away, and the armed escort began to lead the way out of Shapoora.

The long journey to Gandamak was uneventful to the point of tedium. The armed guides soon made it clear that their custody of Bella was protective more than anything else; when no danger threatened they allowed her a great measure of freedom and privacy. They had no fear that she would escape; their function was to ensure that she reached the British camp in safety. And indeed, one look at their ruffianly appearance was generally enough to induce any chance-met band of other tribesmen along the Pass to take flight.

Afghanistan, Bella decided, was surely one of the waste places of the world. Its stony, treeless slopes, its parched soil and whirling sand afforded scant comfort for the traveller. In the evenings, as the colour faded from the umber cliffs and gorges the wind blew fiercely from the Hindu Kush. And this was the country which Resaldar sought to rule when he could have had Haverington Hall for the taking . . .

When they were within a day's ride of Gandamak and the guides spotted a British look-out party ahead, they indicated to Bella, by means of mime, that she was to go ahead alone, and return when her mission had been accomplished. They melted away into the surrounding hills. They knew, as Resaldar had known, that she would not fail to return while her brother Simon was being held at Shapoora.

The non-commissioned officer in charge of the look-out party stared at Bella in astonishment. 'What the devil are you doing out here, son, wandering about on your own?'

'I should,' Bella returned with dignity, 'like to be taken to see Major Cavagnari.'

'Would you, indeed!' He slapped his thigh. '*I* should like to take tea with Her Majesty Queen Victoria. Each of us stands about as much chance of getting his wish as the other!'

Bella chewed her lip. It had not occurred to her, any more than it had occurred to Resaldar, that Army protocol might prevent her from even gaining the ear of the Viceroy's Plenipotentiary.

A thought occurred to her. 'I have a message for him,' she said, 'concerning the whereabouts of the daughter of his friend, General Prewitt.'

'Oh!' The NCO stared at her with heightened interest. 'As a matter of fact, General Prewitt is currently visiting Gandamak, and he's in a rare old state about his daughter. Very well, my lad. You'd better come with me. What's your name?'

'Stanley—' Her mother's maiden name flashed into Bella's mind. 'Fullerton. Stanley Fullerton.'

'Well, come on, Stanley. Follow me.'

Together, they rode to the British camp. It was fortified with lunetes and shelter trenches, and beyond these the officers' tents were pitched. Bella waited outside Major Cavagnari's double-poled tent while the NCO respectfully sought audience with the Viceroy's Plenipotentiary. A little later Bella was commanded to enter the tent.

Major Cavagnari read Resaldar's note, without any change in his expression, and then laid it on the desk before him.

'The note mentions other hostages besides Miss Nicolette Prewitt,' he said. 'You, I take it, are one of those hostages. Why were you chosen to deliver the note, and what was a boy of your age doing in Afghanistan in the first place?'

Bella had already prepared her story. She had no wish to be trapped into revealing her sex to the Army, for she knew that they would then insist on sending another hostage to Shapoora in her place. And she could not endure the thought of kicking her heels at Gandamak while worrying about Simon and wondering what heroics he might be getting up to.

'My half-brother, Simon, and I came to Afghanistan because we learnt that we had a cousin in this country. There was the question, you see, of whether or not Simon was the legitimate heir to the family estate. In any event, Mr Lionel Bromley was helping us to find our cousin, and Miss Prewitt was travelling with our caravan when we were all taken prisoner by Shapoora tribesmen. Resaldar, the Khan of Shapoora, turned out to be the son of the cousin we were seeking.' She added with dignity, 'It is not a relationship which I take any pleasure in acknowledging.'

Major Cavagnari nodded. 'Why did the Khan send *you* with the message stating his demands?'

'Because I am older than Simon, and because he knew that I would not fail to return with your answer while he had my brother in his power.'

'Yes, I see. Very well, young Stanley, go and wait outside.' To the guard at the door of the tent, Major Cavagnari said, 'Convey my respects to Generals Maude and Prewitt, and tell them that I need an urgent audience with them.'

It seemed to Bella that she waited hours while the three officers were in conference inside Major Cavagnari's tent. But at last she was summoned to enter.

A bluff, fresh-faced man of middle age claimed Bella's attention immediately. 'I am General Prewitt. My daughter—tell me, is she safe? The scoundrels have not harmed her?'

'She is quite safe, sir, and is being confined in the women's quarters at Shapoora.'

'That will send her out of her mind! She cannot endure being confined, being bored! It is her nature to seek excitement.' He turned to Major Cavagnari. 'I still say we must send troops at all speed!'

'My dear Clive—' Major Cavagnari began with a mixture of compassion and weary impatience.

Bella was emboldened to interrupt. 'I would urge extreme caution, sir. Some act of aggression will be expected, and Resaldar's men will be on the alert. Perhaps I could draw a sketch plan of Shapoora for you, and that might suggest a possible plan of campaign? And of course, I could make sure that the hotages knew when to expect a raid—'

'No,' Major Cavagnari cut her short. 'No, there will be no raid. General Maude and I are in agreement, and only General Prewitt's natural feelings as a father—however, that is no concern of yours, boy. You will return to your cousin, and tell him that we agree to his demands in principle.'

'*Agree?*' Bella stared at him, dumbfounded.

'Yes, certainly.' The Major turned to General Prewitt, ignoring her. 'You *must* see, Clive, what an advantage it would be to Her Majesty's Government to have a half-English Emir ruling Afghanistan!'

'But the man is a scoundrel—'

'No more so than any of the other claimants to the throne,' General Maude put in cynically.

Bella had found her voice. 'I—I can scarcely believe that the Army really means to give in to blackmail without a struggle—'

'I daresay not,' General Maude responded with tolerant good humour. 'But though you are clearly very advanced for your age, I doubt if you know anything about the politics of this country. Do you, young Stanley Fullerton?'

'No,' Bella was forced to admit.

'The Afghans consist of a ramshackle number of tribes, united in only one thing—their hatred of the British, whom they call White Kaffirs. They hate Christians almost as bitterly, and those two factors have always made it difficult for us to establish a frontier in Afghanistan. So consider how it would benefit us to force the tribes to accept an Emir who is not only half-British, but a Christian to boot!'

'I can't see the tribes accepting a Christian,' General Prewitt put in obstinately. 'I still say—'

'I'm sure the Khan of Shapoora would be prepared to convert to Islam if the prize was the throne of Afghanistan. But at heart he would still be sympathetic to our cause.'

'I don't agree! Nothing could alter the fact that he is half-British, and the tribes would jib at that—'

'In the end,' Major Cavagnari entered the discussion with a sardonic smile, 'the tribes will have to accept the claimant with the strongest military backing. And if we back the Khan of Shapoora they will have to acknowledge him as their Emir, whether they like it or not.'

'But,' Bella said in desperation, 'there are other claimants, surely, with more rights than my cousin—'

'There is no one claimant acceptable to all the tribes,' Major Cavagnari told her. 'Until now the British have backed the claim of Yakoob Khan, the son of the late Shere Ali, as being the best of a bad bunch. But we are becoming more than a little disillusioned with Yakoob Khan. He has shown that he is not to be trusted; we believe that he has been trying to stir up the tribes against the British.

'So,' the Major shrugged, 'if your cousin is willing to come to terms, and if he will grant our demands for a scientific frontier in Afghanistan, with a British Resident in Kabul, then we will withdraw our backing from Yakoob Khan and help your cousin to the throne instead. Tell him that.'

'And make it a condition, at least,' General Prewitt growled, 'that my daughter should be released forthwith!'

'Steady, old man.' Major Cavagnari placed a soothing hand on his friend's arm. 'You can't expect him to relinquish his ace at this early stage in the game. The matter can't be rushed. Yakoob Khan must be seen to be given ample time to come to terms, or the tribes will consider that we have betrayed him, and are not to be trusted.'

'So my poor little girl is to go on languishing in some damned harem for months on end!'

'I'm afraid it can't be helped.' Major Cavagnari turned to Bella. 'Negotiations will have to be entered into for placing your cousin on the throne, and with all due respect, the Army can't negotiate with a schoolboy. Has your cousin no one else of authority and intelligence whom he can send?'

'There is Lionel Bromley,' Bella replied mechanically, 'or Seamus Flynn. But *he*, I believe, is wary of the British Army, because of a matter of selling guns to the Afghans—'

'Yes, I remember him,' General Maude put in with a grim smile. 'But rogue though he is, he would make a fitting conspirator.'

'I'll write a note to him,' Major Cavagnari nodded, 'assuring him that the gun-running matter has been wiped from the record.' He addressed Bella again. 'Tell your cousin to send him to talk terms.' He reached for a handbell on his desk, and rang it. 'You will be given a meal, and will share an officer's tent for the night—'

'No,' Bella said swiftly, and then softened her refusal.

'I should be grateful for the meal, but I would prefer to return afterwards to where the guides are waiting for me in the hills. The sooner I start the return journey, the better.'

In the event, she was not allowed to leave without a pack-horse carrying some trunks containing Nicolette's clothes which General Prewitt insisted on sending to his daughter.

'Her servants, the fools, arrived with it from Bombay, having lost her on the way. It might cheer her to be able to wear some of her pretty things.'

Bella said nothing about the *chador* and veil which Nicolette was being forced to wear, and would most certainly have to go on wearing. She accepted the trunks and left with a heavy heart to rejoin her escort of tribesmen.

It was the bitterest pill to swallow, having to return to Shapoora and tell Resaldar that the Army had given in to his demands without even token resistance. She imagined his blue eyes glowing with triumph, his imperious ways becoming even more gallingly overbearing now that the throne of Afghanistan was within his grasp.

She tried to obliterate his image by thinking of Lionel instead. She had, dutifully, concentrated on thinking of Lionel at least once a day, and now she told herself determinedly that one of the reasons why she had been so careful not to risk being prevented from returning to Shapoora by the Army was to be with him.

The return journey to Shapoora was even more monotonous, for now Bella could not even enliven the tedium by imagining ways in which the Army would shatter her cousin's pretensions. All she had to look forward to, at the end of it, was the distasteful prospect of having to tell Resaldar that he had won.

One late afternoon Bella and her guides took shelter

for the night at a *rabāt*, or frontier post, built along the caravan track. It consisted of a wide, mud-walled ṣquare with a crudely ornamented gateway at the centre of one of its sides. A small mosque had been fashioned in the middle of the open space within the walls. All around the inside of the square, rooms had been constructed for travellers, with a portico leading off each for animals and baggage. Better even than the comparative comfort and privacy which the *rabāt* afforded, Bella discovered that a river ran not far from it, screened by an avenue of willows and thickets of tamarisks.

At dusk the guides would be at their prayers, and no one would see Bella slipping away to the river, to the unaccustomed luxury of a bathe.

Ever since she had begun her masquerade she had had to wash furtively and swiftly as and when she could. But now, in that peaceful, empty spot, with the guards at their devotions, she was able to strip off Simon's breeches and shirt and step into the cool water.

She had just finished washing her hair when she became aware of a change in the light. The sun was setting and reflecting upon the dust in the air, casting over everything a blinding saffron glow.

Bella stood upon a flat rock, stretching her arms above her head, marvelling at the strange effect of the light which made her appear as a naked statue cast in gold.

With a sigh, she came back to earth and stepped from the rock, reaching for the dusty breeches and shirt once more. She was buttoning the shirt when the slightest of movements from among the tamarisks caught her eye.

What had seemed no more than light and shadow among the tamarisks resolved itself into the shape of a man. Her breath caught with fear, and she was about to shout for the guards when the man stepped out of his former concealment.

She was astonished, and then dismayed, by the way in which her heart began to pound as she recognised Resaldar. No longer regally dressed, but looking as much of a brigand as his subjects, his robe was dusty, his tawny-gold head bare and glinting in the yellow light.

Why was she so excited at the unexpected sight of him?

And swiftly on the heels of that thought came one far more disturbing in its implications.

How long had he been standing there, watching her?

CHAPTER
FOUR

RESALDAR MOVED towards Bella, and said casually, 'We seem to be of like mind, Cousin Stanley. While we're bathing you can tell me what transpired at Gandamak.'

Relief coursed through her. He had, after all, only just arrived. He had obviously been too impatient to await her return to Shapoora, and had ridden out to meet her and the tribesmen. He must have left his horse at the *rabāt*, and walked to the river to wash off his dust.

'I have already bathed,' she told him. 'And as for what transpired at Gandamak—Major Cavagnari accepts your proposition, and wishes you to send Flynn to negotiate terms.'

'Good!' But he seemed strangely abstracted, and not alight with triumph as she would have expected. He unfastened his robe, allowing it to slip to the ground. His hard-muscled shoulders and chest glowed like polished bronze in the saffron light. Bella was staring at him, bemused, when she realised that he was about to remove the wide-legged pantaloons which he had been wearing underneath the outer garment. She turned away quickly, the blood surging to her cheeks.

'Sit down, Cousin,' she heard him command, 'and talk to me while I bathe.'

'I—I have to go,' she stammered. 'I—have to attend to my horse.'

She fled before he could question that lame excuse.

Back at the *rabāt*, she tried to regain her equilibrium, and began to rehearse how she could modify Major Cavagnari's message so that it would not seem too complete a triumph for Resaldar.

But when her cousin returned from his bathe he seemed in no hurry to discuss the matter and savour his triumph to the full. He came to stand beside Bella, who was watching the guides broil meat over a large fire which they had built in the centre of the mud-walled square.

'I trust, Cousin,' Resaldar murmured, 'that your horse has benefited from your attentions.'

'My horse? Oh—oh, yes.' She gave him a startled look.

He said something to the guides, and turned to her again. 'We shall dine together in private. I daresay you have chosen a room for yourself in the *rabāt*. Pray lead me to it, Cousin, and my men will serve us there.'

She could think of no objection to raise, and led the way to the farthest corner of the square where she had selected a room for herself.

Resaldar's glance fell upon the trunks which General Prewitt had insisted she take to Shapoora. 'And what are those?' he wanted to know.

Bella explained that they contained Nicolette's clothes. He knelt beside one of the trunks and took from it a gown of palest gold Surah silk, with a low-cut, closely gathered bodice goffered at intervals with Breton lace and a narrow, trained skirt which was adorned with large padded puffs on each hip.

'Do women in England,' Resaldar demanded, '*really* wear this sort of garment?'

'Indeed they do,' Bella assured him.

'I had no notion. Miss Prewitt, when she arrived at Shapoora, was wearing a sari . . .'

'She had been separated from her servants and her luggage,' Bella explained, a little amused by his naive wonder, 'and was obliged to accept the offer of a sari at one of the *dāk* houses where we stopped.'

'I should,' Resaldar said thoughtfully, 'very much like to see this being worn. I can hardly believe that any human shape is capable of being tortured into such a confining garment.'

'Perhaps Miss Prewitt would consent to model it for you,' Bella suggested.

He shook his head. 'It would be considered quite shocking in the harem.' He gave Bella a speculative look. 'You are of slight build, Cousin Stanley. Perhaps *you* could—'

Bella had stiffened. To her relief, they were joined at that moment by tribesmen who hurried to wait upon them. *Numdahs*—small Afghan carpets—were unrolled and placed upon the mud floor for them to sit upon, and a table of crude construction had been obtained from somewhere. Broiled meat and *chapattis* were carried in and placed upon it.

Resaldar had still not mentioned the Viceroy's Plenipotentiary, or asked to be told of his capitulation in detail. His mood had become abstracted once more, but sometimes when he glanced at Bella his blue eyes held a strange glitter which she found disturbing without being able to explain its significance.

At last, when their meal came to an end, Bella felt impelled to bring the subject up herself. 'Since you took the trouble to ride out and meet us, Cousin, you must surely be eager to know exactly what transpired at Gandamak. Major Cavagnari is of the opinion that it would suit the British to have a half-English Emir on the throne of Afghanistan. Obviously, you will be no more than a puppet of the British Government, but if you choose to regard it as a triumph—'

'Yes, I regard it as a triumph,' he said, unperturbed, and spoke to one of the hovering tribesmen. A leather flask was brought to him, together with two beakers of animal horn. The guides withdrew, leaving Bella alone with Resaldar.

He unscrewed the top of the flask, and filled the beakers with an opaque white liquid. 'We shall drink to my future as the Emir of Kabul, Cousin,' he said, setting one of the beakers before her.

She picked it up, studying its contents. 'What is it?'

'*Fulloodeh*. A liquor illegally distilled from wheat. And very potent indeed, I might add.'

'I should prefer some tea,' Bella said, setting the beaker down on the board.

'What a prim, missish response!' Resaldar mocked. 'Come, Cousin, I insist that you drink with me. It's time you were introduced to some of the male vices.'

'I really would prefer not to—' Bella began.

'And I insist.'

That disquieting glitter was back in his eyes again, and she had an uneasy feeling that he might well try to force the liquor down her throat with the help of the tribesmen. Judging it prudent to capitulate, she raised the beaker to her mouth, and found the liquor over-sweet, with an unfamiliar after-taste.

'To the throne of Kabul!' she heard Resaldar say as he, too, drank of the *fulloodeh*, draining his beaker. He refilled it, and said, 'Drink up, Cousin, and let me pour you another.'

She tilted her beaker unobtrusively as she lifted it, so that much of its contents ran down the side and quickly became absorbed by the mud floor.

It was growing dark, making it easier for her to dispose of the liquor with which Resaldar continually refilled her beaker, pouring it away on the floor. He called for candles and for another flask of *fulloodeh*, and then dismissed the tribesmen for the night.

While Bella had successfully avoided taking more than a few sips of the liquor, Resaldar was becoming alarmingly inebriated, his conversation more and more unrestrained. Several times she suggested that it was growing late, and that he should retire to his own quarters.

'The night is young, Cousin,' Resaldar slurred, and refilled their beakers again. He held his aloft in a toast. 'Now, what shall we drink to this time? I know—to the ladies!'

He leant confidentially towards Bella. 'I daresay you are an innocent where the ladies are concerned, Cousin. Well, I mean to rectify that, and take your education in hand. When we return to Shapoora, you shall have your pick of the harem!'

'I find this conversation most distasteful,' Bella said stiffly.

He waved an admonitory finger at her. 'You must guard against a certain prudishness in your nature, Cousin Stanley! However, for the sake of your puritanical conscience, it shall all be done most properly. You will marry the young woman you select from the harem!'

'You are being quite outrageous!'

'No, no,' he enunciated carefully. 'The marriage will not be binding, have no fear! It will last only while you remain at Shapoora. I know what you are thinking, Cousin. You are thinking that the arrangement would not be fair to the young woman. But this is not England, you know—'

'No, indeed!'

He ignored the scathing interruption. 'The women of Shapoora came originally from Kafiristan, and there it was the tradition for females to be treated as slaves, bought and sold like household goods.' He nodded owlishly, pleased with himself. 'Yes, you will be married in accordance with the old traditions of Kafiristan. I shall buy your bride from her father, and a goat will be sacrificed, and you will then be considered man and wife just for as long as it pleases you, Cousin Stanley.'

Bella jumped to her feet. 'Since *you* will not leave, I shall select another room for myself. Good night!'

He lurched to his feet too, blocking her way. 'Before you go, Cousin Stanley,' he said with a leer, 'you must indulge my whim to see that fine English gown modelled, if only by a girlish youth.'

'No!'

He had taken her by the shoulders. 'I shall help you. Never fear, between us we should contrive not to be too clumsy with the delicate fabric.'

His hand began to fumble with the buttons of her shirt. Her cheeks flaming, Bella tried to fight him off and felt the shirt tear under his hands. Desperately striving to clutch the tatters to her, she cried,

'You hateful, depraved brute! You're drunk!'

'*I am no more drunk*,' he said in a voice which was suddenly cold and sharp as a whiplash, '*than you are my boy cousin Stanley*!'

'You're—talking nonsense. Of course you're drunk— you have been drinking all evening—'

'*Fulloodeh*,' he said curtly, 'is a non-alcoholic liquor strained from wheat, and mixed with snow-water and sherbet.'

Bella drew a sharp breath. 'Then—it was all a char-ade! This whole evening—oh, how disgustingly deceitful of you!'

'I should not,' he said in an ominous voice, 'talk of deceitfulness if I were you, Cousin. If you *are*, indeed, my cousin, and that was not also a lie. What is your name?'

'Arabella. I am generally called Bella, and I *am* your cousin—unfortunately.' A slow flush stained her cheeks. 'I suppose—you must have seen me bathing in the river after all . . .'

'Yes, I saw you.' He glanced at her, and looked away. 'I decided to punish you a little.'

His gaze returned to her, and rested on her right shoulder which had been left naked by the tattered shirt. He made an angry sound and stooped, grabbing the gown of Surah silk from Nicolette Prewitt's trunk. 'Here,' he said brusquely. 'Take it. For the sake of decency, go into the portico and put it on!'

She could have refused, and changed instead into one of Simon's spare shirts which she had with her. It would certainly have been quicker and simpler, and she could have argued that nothing would look more absurd and incongruous than Nicolette's gown teamed with Simon's sturdy boots. But for some reason which she did not understand she suddenly *wanted* to wear a frivolous gown which underlined her femininity.

It was impossible, too, not to take pleasure in the luxurious feel of the silk as she slipped into the gown. It fitted her to perfection, the narrow, trained skirt flattering her slender thighs, the padded panniers on the hips emphasising her small waist. She was glad that her hair had grown a little during the journey to Gandamak, and was no longer quite so short and boyish. She ran her fingers through her curls, and then, her heart beating with a mixture of emotions, she returned bare-footed to the room to face Resaldar.

If her appearance impressed or pleased him, he gave no sign of it. 'Why did you embark on such a charade?' he demanded.

'When Simon and I first joined Lionel Bromley, it was suggested that we would be less conspicuous in the Khyber Pass if I pretended to be a youth. Then, when we were brought to Shapoora—well, I had no intention of being banished to the harem like Nicolette Prewitt.'

'That,' he said grimly, 'is precisely where you will be going the moment we return to Shapoora!'

'No!'

'Have you any conception,' he asked harshly, 'of the danger you courted by allowing yourself to be sent to Gandamak? Good God, I was concerned enough about you when I believed you to be a young boy. If I had known that you were a *girl*—'

'You were concerned about me, Cousin?' Bella asked softly, her heart giving an odd little flutter. Heavens, she thought with astonishment, I am being positively coquettish. It must be the influence of Nicolette's gown . . .

'I was sufficiently concerned,' she heard Resaldar say, 'to leave Shapoora soon after you did, and to keep a watchful eye on you from a distance.'

'You really did that?' She thought of him trailing after herself and the tribesmen, running the appalling risk of taking on any of his chance-met enemies single-handed. 'I was never in any danger, Resaldar.'

His voice roughened. 'I told you something of the way in which Infidels regard women. In spite of the veneer of religion they acquired when they converted to the Muslim faith, that is still fundamentally how they regard them. My blood runs cold when I contemplate what might have happened if *they* had chanced to see you bathing in the river!'

She remembered her pose in the saffron light, her arms stretched above her head, and flushed. She said in a muffled voice, 'It was quite odious of you to spy on me from the shadows. Your behaviour tonight has been odious from start to finish. If you had any gentlemanly instincts at all, Resaldar, you would go away and leave me in peace now that you have had your revenge.'

'I have never claimed to be a gentleman,' he said, but he began to move to the doorway. Then he stopped, and looked at her. In the guttering light of the candles his face had acquired an enigmatic expression, and his eyes were mysterious, unreadable hollows.

'Would that frothy creation,' he asked unexpectedly, 'be a ball gown?'

'Oh no. A ball gown would be far more magnificent.'

'It hardly seems possible,' he said, shaking his head.

'I assure you, it's true. A ball gown would be made of satin and lace, perhaps, and trimmed with flounces and ribbons and small bouquets of flowers.'

'My father used to tell me of balls which he had attended as a young British officer,' Resaldar mused. 'I understand that men and women dance together at them. There is something called a waltz, is there not?'

Bella nodded, amused and a little touched by his ignorance of the civilised world.

Resaldar hesitated. 'I think,' he said abruptly, 'that the Emir of Kabul might well be expected to waltz. Do you know how to waltz, Cousin Bella?'

'Oh yes.'

'Then perhaps you would not object to showing me how it is done.'

This was, Bella thought bemusedly, a strange evening indeed, and one she would not lightly forget. Aloud, she said, 'Very well. Watch carefully.'

Lifting the hem of the gown so that he could follow the movements of her bare feet, she hummed a tune and demonstrated the steps of the waltz.

'Now let us try it together,' Bella said. 'You must put your right arm about my waist.'

Frowning, he moved towards her. 'It seems an immodest manner of dancing.'

'Nevertheless, it is how it is done.'

His arm was stiff and self-conscious about her waist at first. But he had a natural aptitude and an inborn sense of rhythm, and after a few moments he relaxed and began to whirl her authoritatively around the small room. Bella laughed up at him, and started to sing aloud the words of the popular ballad she had been humming:

> *Come, oh sweetheart, while the morning*
> *Glistens gladness with its kiss.*
> *While the sun's approaching fullness*
> *And our natures feel that this*
> *Is the time for love that's sowing*
> *Seeds for flowers of brightest glowing* . . .

She felt Resaldar's hand tighten about her own, and glanced up at him. The song died on her lips. In the light of the candles his blue eyes held a disturbing expression. Simultaneously they stopped dancing. He released her, dropping his arms to his sides. But neither of them moved away. Their glances were locked in wordless communication. Abruptly, he stretched out a hand and laid it upon her throat, his fingers slightly unsteady as they moved over her skin. Then with a sudden urgency he drew her close against him. His lips fastened on hers with hunger and explosive passion, and she could feel the wild beating of his heart through the thin material of Nicolette's gown. She clung to him, swept along by emotions totally unfamiliar to her.

He released her abruptly, and without a word strode to the door. She raised her hands to her flushed cheeks, and stood there for a long while before it occurred to her to prepare for bed.

She did not sleep. She was consumed by a physical ache for Resaldar. *So this is what it is like*, she thought. *This strange sweet pain . . .*

How could she wean him away from his mad, vainglorious scheme to become the Emir of Kabul, and persuade him to take up the rôle of master of Haverington Hall instead, with herself by his side?

And if it proved impossible, could she consider making her home in this windswept, sunbaked alien land to be with him? Yes—yes, she could. There was no sacrifice she could not make for his sake.

How, she thought with wonder, could she ever have contemplated marrying Lionel? She would have to tell him, as soon as she returned to Shapoora, that she could not accept his proposal.

In the morning, after some hesitation, Bella dressed once more in Simon's breeches and shirt. For one thing, she found the thought of wearing Nicolette's clothes distasteful; for another, she did not know whether or not Resaldar intended to tell the tribesmen at this stage that she was a woman.

Whatever Resaldar's reaction might have been when he saw her emerge from her room in breeches and shirt, he did not show it. His expression was totally blank, his eyes empty of expression. He made no reference whatever to the scene which had taken place between them, but merely gave her a curt good morning. Bella was puzzled and hurt by his manner, and could think of no explanation for it.

He sought her out only once, after they had breakfasted, and that was merely to make her repeat in detail all that Major Cavagnari had said.

'So,' he exploded when she had finished. 'The British propose to wait on Yakoob Khan before they accede to my demands! Are they crazy? Of course my uncle will come to terms! He is so anxious to succeed Shere Ali as Emir that he had his elder brother, my uncle Ibrahim Khan, imprisoned and killed!'

Bella forgot her hurt, and the distance which he had been placing between them, and thought only of his safety. 'Resaldar,' she burst out, 'won't you please abandon your ambition to become Emir? If your uncle Yakoob Khan is as ruthless as you say, and he gets wind of your plans he could be extremely dangerous to you—'

Resaldar raised his eyebrows at her, and said in a cold voice, 'I am fully alive to all the dangers. Yakoob Khan is not the only one who would wish me out of the way if he got wind of the fact that the British have a strong motive for putting me on the throne. All the other claimants would try to eliminate me—my cousins Hamid Khan and Achmed Isa, for instance. Even old Wali Mahomed, my great-uncle . . .' He gave an angry laugh. 'Flynn must make it clear to the British that I don't intend waiting on the whim of Yakoob Khan. If they wish to see the hostages alive, they will have to act without delay!'

'I don't,' Bella said softly, 'believe that you will do any of the hostages any harm, Resaldar, no matter how the British may behave.'

He gave her a disconcerting look in which there seemed to be active hostility and dislike. 'Don't you?' he returned coldly, and walked away.

Bella thought she was beginning to understand the reason behind his chilly, inimical attitude towards her. That explosion of passion between them had rendered him vulnerable, and if he wished to pursue his ambitions to grab the throne of Kabul he could not afford vulnerability. So, by treating her with distant enmity, he was seeking to put her back upon an impersonal plane again, where she was no more than a hostage.

That he was not succeeding she knew by the haunted expression in his eyes sometimes when she chanced to discover his gaze upon her. But not once, during the rest of the journey back to Shapoora, did he allow himself to be alone with her again, and when he addressed her at all it was in curt monosyllables.

As soon as they reached Shapoora, Resaldar called on Flynn to join him inside the Khan's residence for a conference. Bella was ignored. She shrugged, and went to meet Simon and Lionel, who were hurrying towards her from the domed house.

They could scarcely believe that the Viceroy's Plenipotentiary had agreed to Resaldar's demands.

'Although,' Lionel said reflectively, 'I can well see how it might suit the British to have a puppet on the throne.'

'Resaldar a puppet?' Simon scoffed, his eyes alight with hero worship. 'I wager that our cousin will be nothing of the sort!'

'There is something else,' Bella said, changing the subject. 'Resaldar has discovered that I am a girl.' She felt herself blushing, and half-turned away.

'I must own that I'm glad!' Lionel exclaimed. 'I could not have endured seeing you sent on any other perilous journeys!'

'Yes, well,' Bella shrugged, 'it also means that Resaldar intends banishing me to the harem. He seems to have temporarily forgotten about it, but I have no doubt that it will come back to him soon.' She lifted her chin. 'He will find that I do not go quite as easily as Nicolette Prewitt.'

A black-robed woman arrived from the harem with

hot water, and Bella excused herself and went to her own partition in the house to wash. Afterwards, discarding Simon's breeches and shirt, she dressed in one of her own gowns. It was not nearly as elegant as the creation of Surah silk borrowed from Nicolette, but studying her reflection in the mirror Bella thought that she looked well enough. She threaded a matching green ribbon through her curls, and awaited a summons from Resaldar.

It came soon afterwards. Her heart beating fast, she followed the servant to the Khan's residence.

Flynn was with Resaldar when she arrived. The Irishman's eyes widened at sight of her in a look of appreciation, and she could almost see him wondering how he might possibly exploit her newly discovered femininity to his own advantage.

'You may leave us, Flynn,' Resaldar said imperiously, and the Irishman rose.

Bella seated herself, uninvited, and gazed steadily at Resaldar. 'I cannot, of course, prevent you from having me conveyed to the harem by force,' she began, 'But as for the *chador*, I positively refuse—'

'I am not sending you to the harem.'

'Oh?' She gave him a puzzled frown. 'But you said—'

'I have changed my mind.'

Bella waited for him to continue. He, too, had bathed and discarded his dusty clothes, and was once more magnificently robed. A sapphire stone in his head-dress almost matched his eyes. Bella's heart contracted with an emotion that was half pain as she looked at him.

He met her eyes in an expressionless glance. 'A house will be put at your disposal in the village.'

Joy quickened inside her. It could only mean, she thought, that he could not bear to hide her away in the harem, where they would never see one another.

'You will,' she heard him go on, 'be joined by Miss Prewitt.'

'Oh . . .' Bella felt slightly deflated, and then realised that he could hardly make such an exception for herself alone without exciting comment among his tribesmen.

'The Princess Fawzia,' she heard Resaldar continue, 'will leave the harem, and will live with you and Miss Prewitt.'

Fawzia, Bella thought, confused. The princess of the Hazara tribe, of whom Resaldar had shown such a curious reluctance to talk in the past . . .

'Why?' she asked bluntly.

He rose, and began to pace the floor. When he replied it was seemingly at a tangent. 'I learnt very little of the ways of the British from my father. My mother, Shazeen, taught me about life in the Emir's palace, of the conventions and the customs which obtain there. It was she, more than anyone or anything else, who awakened my sense of dynasty, and determined me to seize the throne of Kabul if I could . . .'

His voice tailed off. Bella broke the silence which followed. 'Resaldar, *why* is Fawzia living at Shapoora if she is a princess of another tribe?'

'Her father sent her here,' he replied without inflection. 'The Khan of the Hazaras is my ally.' As before, he seemed reluctant to be drawn on the subject of Fawzia, for he continued, 'As I've said, I know little of the British social customs, and since my position as Emir will inevitably bring me into close contact with prominent members of British society, it is necessary to learn the rudiments.'

'You wish us to teach you?' Bella asked with a frown.

'No.' He looked away from her. 'I wish you to teach Fawzia all that should be known about social behaviour in Britain.' Now he met Bella's eyes, and something entered his own—a look of torment and hastily sup-pressed desire. 'You will not, however,' he went on almost inaudibly, 'teach her the waltz. I have decided that waltzing will not be allowed at the Palace.'

A sick certainty had been growing inside Bella. She asked quietly—'*Why* did Fawzia's father send her to Shapoora, Resaldar?'

'She is to be my wife,' his bleak voice put into words Bella's fears. 'When I am Emir of Kabul, Fawzia will be my consort.'

CHAPTER
FIVE

BELLA SAT utterly still, concentrating on keeping her expression impassive so that Resaldar would not be aware of the chaos of pain and loss which his revelation had thrown her into.

Then the spirit which had enabled her to survive so many years of Great-Uncle Howard's tyranny came to her aid, and she thought defiantly—*I won't give up so easily*!

He couldn't love Fawzia. Even if Bella did not have the bitter-sweet memory of his mouth upon her own, of her body crushed against his in a turbulent eruption of passion, his reluctance to speak about Fawzia would have told her so.

No, it was obviously an arranged marriage. Fawzia's father would support Resaldar's claim to the throne of Afghanistan in return for the honour of seeing his daughter installed as consort. But if Resaldar did not become Emir after all, the chief of the Hazaras would look elsewhere for an alliance.

Bella tightened her hands into determined fists. Resaldar's bid for the throne was crazy. If he couldn't give it up voluntarily, she herself would do what she could to thwart him. He must be made to see that there was far more waiting for him in happiness and fulfilment as the master of Haverington Hall in England than there ever would be as ruler over an arid, ramshackle country like Afghanistan.

Aloud, she said with deliberate provocation, 'Fawzia is obviously a cautious young lady. She waits in the wings until you have been proclaimed Emir. It does not suit her, perhaps, to risk being no more than the wife of the Khan of Shapoora—'

'You are impertinent, Cousin!' Resaldar rapped. His eyes had become narrow blue slits and his voice was icy. 'I will not permit Fawzia to be disparaged!'

'Well, that is how it strikes me,' Bella said defiantly, but she had been badly jolted by his swift and passionate defence of the girl.

'That is because you are ignorant! The only reason why Fawzia is not yet my wife is because of our different religions.'

'Oh . . . She is a Muslim, I suppose?'

'Yes. It will be necessary for one of us to convert.'

Was there a spark of hope there? Aloud, Bella probed, 'And neither of you is eager to do so?'

'It is not as simple as that. Fawzia is quite prepared to adopt the Christian faith. But I may have to convert to Islam instead. Until we are sure which it is to be, we must postpone the marriage.'

Bella stared at him. 'And when will you be sure, Resaldar?'

He shrugged. 'When I have been proclaimed Emir of Kabul, and have tested the reaction of the various tribes to my continuing as a Christian.'

'It all sounds very clinical and dispassionate to me,' Bella observed tartly. 'You cannot be a very committed Christian if you are considering converting to Islam as a matter of expediency. And you cannot be a very ardent lover if you are willing to postpone your marriage indefinitely—'

'You know nothing whatever about the matter!' He

rose and caught her angrily by the shoulders. She looked into his face, and the pressure of his fingers altered and became an involuntary caress. Bella was shaken and appalled by her own explosive, almost primitive response. She knew now without a doubt that he returned her feelings and did not love Fawzia, and the waste of it all made her lash out at him, trying to punish him with words.

'One thing I do know, Resaldar!' she said bitingly. 'You are so obsessed with the pomp and glory of the throne, with the thought of the power you would wield as Emir, that you're prepared to sacrifice everything to that end!'

'You are quite wrong,' he responded quietly. He moved away from Bella and began to pace the floor as he spoke. 'You said that I was not a committed Christian, and that is true. How could I be? The fact of my Christianity is an accident, because a missionary chanced to be on hand when I was born. If that hadn't been so, I would have been both illegitimate and a heathen. Would that have made me worth any less as a human being? I don't believe it! It has long seemed to me that religion, or the intolerance which it appears to breed, is the root cause of the problems which are rife in my country!'

He faced Bella, his eyes blazing with passion. 'If I am committed to anything, it is to Afghanistan! I want to bring an end to intolerance and warring between the tribes. I want to bring an end to ignorance and savagery. Do you know by what nickname my grandfather, Shere Ali, was known to his subjects? *Dewena*. The madman. He ruled by fear. His authority was based upon dumb terror inspired by hideous and dramatic punishments. But he was only following a long tradition. An Emir has always felt it necessary to be merciless, and to rule by cowing the tribes. I want to put an end to that tradition.'

Bella's heart had begun to beat painfully in her breast as she listened to him. He was not, after all, driven by some vainglorious desire to grab power and position for himself. The depth and passion of his motives, his commitment to Afghanistan, would not permit him to be deflected from the course he had set himself.

He spoke more quietly now, but with no less fervour. 'If possible I should prefer to remain a Christian, as a symbol to the tribes, demonstrating that we can all live peaceably together whatever our creed. I want to promote equality and tolerance between Muslim and Hindu and Christian and Jew. If this tolerance had existed I would not have been driven to persuade the tribesmen of Shapoora to convert to Islam. They were so preoccupied with killing Muslims, or preventing Muslims from killing *them*, that they were in danger of extinction. But if that kind of sectarian hatred and intolerance could be removed, I don't see why even the Infidels should not be left in peace, to worship Imra the Creator and Gish, the War God, if they choose to.'

Bella was silent. She could not quarrel with his sentiments, but at the same time she could not help but feel that he was striving for the impossible. The world was not yet ready for the kind of tolerance which he preached. Perhaps it never would be.

He took her hand in his, and gazed deep into her eyes. 'I know I have no right to ask it of you,' he said quietly. 'But—if Fawzia does convert to Christianity, then as my wife she will be plunged into a world wholly unfamiliar to her. Will you do what you can to prepare her for the changes she must expect?'

'I—will,' Bella said with pain, forcing the words from her numb lips.

He brought her hand briefly to his mouth. Then he

turned away, and tugged at the bell-rope. Flynn, who must have been hovering at the head of the stairs, entered. 'Please conduct my cousin to the house which has been prepared for the ladies,' Resaldar said.

As Bella left with the Irishman, the latter sketched a salaam in Resaldar's direction, and murmured, *'Zendeh bashi.'*

Bella thought there had been a hint of irony in his voice. 'What does that mean?' she enquired.

'It means—*may you live for ever.*' The Irishman grinned. ''Tis an unrealistic sentiment, would you not say, Miss Stanley, considerin' all the many other claimants to the throne who will be wishin' him dead.'

She shivered. If any of Resaldar's relatives should succeed in assassinating him, she thought it would not be long before Flynn, the opportunist, offered to transfer his allegiance to the assassin instead.

In silence she accompanied him to a house with a pointed archway and a wooden door decorated with ritualistic signs, a visual reminder of the villagers' earlier worship of Pagan gods.

A veiled woman servant led them into a room furnished with charpoys and embroidered cushions. Nicolette Prewitt, looking elegant and beautiful in one of the gowns sent by her father, sat on a charpoy. Seated on a cushion opposite her was a girl dressed in a black *chador*. Bella had no more than a swift impression of smooth dark hair and ivory-coloured skin before the girl hurriedly draped a black veil about her head.

'Mr Flynn,' Nicolette demanded, ignoring Bella. 'For how much longer am I to be kept in this accursed village?'

'Whisht, me darlin',' he soothed. 'Have a little patience. Did I not keep me promise, and rescue you from the harem?'

'Yes, and I'm not ungrateful.' Nicolette's angry hauteur melted a little as she regarded the Irishman. It was on the tip of Bella's tongue to assure the girl that Flynn had had nothing to do with Resaldar's decision that she should leave the harem. But Nicolette was speaking again.

'Fawzia has told me all about that upstart Khan's impudent schemes, and I understand that the Army has agreed to his demands. Well, of course I knew they would; Papa would do anything in his power to secure my release, and he is not without influence. But now that the Army has agreed, why can't *I* be set free? The Khan would still have three hostages, and the Army does not go back on its word—'

'Ah, but 'tis desolate *I* would be, Miss Prewitt, were I to be deprived of yer sweet loveliness one day sooner than need be!'

The man's easy charm and lavish compliments were actually having an effect on Nicolette, Bella noted cynically. Then she ignored their exchange and turned her attention to Fawzia.

The girl sat so still in her all-enveloping *chador* and veil that she might have been a statue. Only her eyes, dark and slanted, were exposed, but she kept them averted for most of the time. It was impossible to form an impression of what she was like.

Flynn took his leave, and only now did Nicolette deign to favour Bella with the scantest interest. 'Strange that I never realised you were a female,' she commented.

Bella smiled faintly. It was not strange at all. Nicolette had never been sufficiently interested in anyone but herself to give her fellow travellers a second thought.

'Of course, it was easy for *you* to pass as a boy,' Nicolette added with insulting frankness. 'If you had been a beauty, it would have been another matter. *I* wouldn't have fooled anyone for an instant.'

A woman servant entered with green tea and small cakes. Fawzia removed her veil now that there was no danger of being beheld by male eyes, and Bella saw that she had the slightly flattish features common to the Asian of Mongol ancestry, and a grave, pensive expression.

'You'!' Nicolette addressed the woman servant. 'Fetch my shawl from the room next door.'

The woman looked at her without comprehension. 'Oh, for heaven's sake!' Nicolette snapped at Fawzia. 'You tell her!'

The girl who was destined to become Resaldar's consort turned a look of immense dignity on Nicolette. 'I am a princess of the Hazaras, Miss Prewitt,' she said quietly, in the same inflectionless English with which Resaldar spoke. 'And a descendant of Genghis Khan. I do not relay orders.'

'Well!' Nicolette gasped indignantly. 'A princess indeed! What do you imagine *that* signifies outside this benighted country?' She turned to Bella. '*You* fetch my shawl, will you. I'm tired of arguing and I'm growing chilled.'

'It hasn't,' Bella enquired mildly, without stirring, 'occurred to you to fetch it yourself?'

Nicolette gave her a look of outrage and dislike. Then, grimly acknowledging defeat, she flung herself from the room. Fawzia spoke in a quiet voice.

'It was a great relief to the women when it was learnt that Miss Prewitt would be leaving the harem.'

'Yes, I imagine it was.' Bella hesitated. 'You speak English very well. Did Resaldar teach you?'

Fawzia inclined her head. 'He did.'

'That surprises me. I thought—well, I was under the impression that the sexes were very strictly segregated, even when they are—betrothed.'

'It was necessary for me to learn English,' Fawzia explained with dignity, 'and Resaldar Khan was the only one qualified to teach me. But we were chaperoned by my servants at all times, and I always wore the veil.'

An astonishing thought struck Bella. 'Has Resaldar ever seen you without the veil?' she demanded.

'He saw me once, six years ago, when I was twelve.'

Bella caught her lower lip between her teeth. After a moment she changed the subject. 'You know why I am here, don't you?'

'I do.'

'I suppose I'll have to address you as Your Highness—'

Fawzia's grave, impassive face softened in a brief smile. 'That will not be necessary. We shall be cousins one day. I suggest that you call me Fawzia, and I shall call you Bella.'

'Very well.' Bella studied her. 'Won't you mind sacrificing your religion?'

Fawzia shrugged resignedly. 'I shall mind very much. But my first duty is to Resaldar Khan.'

Bella shook her head in bafflement. Perhaps, because of the difference in their two cultures, it was impossible for her to fathom the workings of Fawzia's mind. It was impossible, too, to feel any jealousy or resentment towards such a submissive, dispassionate girl. A girl whose face Resaldar had only seen once, when she was still a child, and whom he had never held in his arms . . .

'If you do convert to Christianity,' Bella began, 'and you and Resaldar—' She halted, and formed the words with difficulty '. . . are married—you will have to become accustomed to life without the veil. You will be required to meet and converse with perfectly strange men, and live an altogether far more exposed and public life than as a Muslim wife.'

Fawzia listened patiently as Bella sketched for her a picture of what her rôle would be in a Christian marriage. It was difficult to gauge her reaction, for her face remained largely expressionless. But she seemed far more interested in the dogma of the Christian faith than in social customs, and asked searching theological questions which Bella was unable to answer. She also seemed disappointed at the lack of daily ritual in Christian life, and dismayed that there were few penances, such as regular fasting, exacted of one.

When noises reached them from outside, Fawzia excused herself and went to one of the loopholes to look out. 'Come and see,' she invited Bella. 'It is the blessing of the camels, because today is Thursday—the Muslim equivalent of your Saturday, for it is the eve of the Holy day.'

Outside, the camels were being driven back to the village from their grazing. The Koran, folded in a turban and held aloft, suspended between two lances, formed an arch beneath which each beast was forced to pass.

'It protects them from sickness and other evils,' Fawzia explained. 'Do Christians have a similar ceremony, perhaps?'

'No,' Bella was forced to admit, and came to the conclusion that Fawzia would miss the symbolism, the rites and the taboos of Islam far more than she would miss her actual religion when she converted.

The days took on a tenor which was only slightly less monotonous than life in the harem would have been. Flynn had left for Gandamak to negotiate with the Army, and everyone was aware of marking time until he returned.

The house was little more than a prison for the three girls. No one came to visit them, and because their western dress and uncovered faces attracted so much attention—either hostile or unpleasantly lewd—from the village men both Nicolette and Bella felt discouraged from leaving the house. Fawzia accepted conditions with the same willing resignation as she had accepted the confines of the harem, and remained contained and impassive; Nicolette vented her boredom and irritation on anyone who happened to be near, and Bella found herself daily watching the Khan's residence for a glimpse of Resaldar, her longing for him an almost unendurable physical ache.

One evening, while the tribesmen were at their devotions, Bella slipped out briefly to call on Lionel Bromley and Simon in the domed house, and reproached them for their aloofness.

'Don't blame us!' Lionel protested. 'Your cousin hasn't exactly forbidden us to call, but he has nevertheless left us with a very strong impression that the house where you are living is out of bounds.'

'I daresay,' Simon defended, as ever loyal to his hero Resaldar, 'it is out of consideration for his fiancée. She is not accustomed to male visitors.'

'*His fiancée*,' Bella echoed, amazed at the fresh pain which could be generated by putting a perfectly well-known fact into words. But the conversation had given her a sudden inspiration.

'Resaldar arranged for us to live together so that Fawzia could learn something about social intercourse in a Christian society,' she said. 'That must surely include practising the art of conversing with male visitors!'

She hurried to share her idea with Fawzia and Nicolette. 'I think it's time for Fawzia to put into practice something of what she has learnt about western ways. We'll arrange a dinner party and invite the men!'

Nicolette hunched her shoulders sullenly, and looked bored. Bella guessed that she would have displayed more enthusiasm if Flynn had not still been away at Gandamak.

'Until I convert—if I *do* convert—' Fawzia pointed out, 'I remain bound by Islamic law. I could not appear without the veil, and I could not dine in male company.'

'I hadn't thought of that,' Bella said, dismayed.

As always, Fawzia demonstrated her complete lack of self-interest. 'You have set your heart on this,' she told Bella, 'and I shall, therefore, take my meal separately, attended by my maid-servants, and join you afterwards.'

Bella threw herself enthusiastically into arrangements for the dinner party, and sent one of the servants with invitations to Resaldar, Simon and Lionel. Using such provisions as she found at hand, she braised chicken with wild onions and apricots, and set the servants to baking bread. She improvised a pudding, using a local sweet-meat called *talkhan*, a kind of cake made of dried mulberries and walnuts.

Resaldar had accepted the invitation with polite thanks but no comment, Lionel and Simon with expressions of delight. Bella dressed early, hesitating over the limited choice which her wardrobe offered. Finally, mindful of the fact that Fawzia, in whose honour the party was being held, would have no choice at all but would merely be wearing a *chador* and veil of silk instead of homespun, she chose a sober gown of dark-blue foulard.

Nicolette had scorned to change for the occasion, until she saw the two other girls. Then, with a malicious smile, she disappeared and did not return until the guests were being greeted.

Bella was welcoming Resaldar, her heart beating tempestuously as she studied him. He wore loose *shālvar* trousers of cream silk, together with a richly embroidered jacket which fastened high at the neck, like a mandarin's coat. His head-dress was of deep-blue silk which lent an intensity of colour to his eyes, and one end of which fell in luxurious folds to his shoulder.

He was murmuring something conventional in response to Bella's greeting when Nicolette made her entrance and positioned herself so that she would form as sharp a contrast as possible with the two other girls. Bella felt Resaldar stiffen. Her hand, over which he had been bowing, was enclosed in a painful grip, and an under-current of passion flashed between them, so strong that she marvelled at the fact that no one else seemed aware of it.

Nicolette had changed into her gown of gold Surah silk. She could have had no way of guessing that the gown, which she had chosen only in order to put the two other girls firmly in the shade, would have such powerful, evocative memories for Bella and Resaldar. As their glances went to Nicolette and then locked once again in hopeless anguish, both of them were remembering the night in the *rabāt*, when Bella had worn the gown and had taught him the waltz.

It was Fawzia who broke the spell. Heavily veiled though she was, she approached with all the self-assurance of a western hostess and put into practice some of the social graces which Bella had been teaching her by offering Resaldar a drink of sherbet.

The evening became a blur to Bella. She was vaguely aware that Lionel cast many an ardent glance in her direction, and that he took the opportunity, after dinner, to engage her in conversation, but she could never afterwards remember the subjects they had discussed.

Resaldar was the first to leave the party. After complimenting Fawzia on the grace with which she had coped with her first rôle as hostess to western guests, he turned to Bella, and added somewhat curtly,

'I should like a private word with you, Cousin, if you please.'

Bella accompanied him to the door, and closed it behind them. He waved away two hovering servants, and spoke abruptly.

'How does Fawzia *really* feel about breaking such long-held taboos?'

'I think she is sustained by a sense of duty towards you.' Bella hesitated. 'I don't think she expects to be happy, or contented, or fulfilled. She expects only to serve and to obey.

'Yes,' he agreed bleakly. His glance searched Bella's face. 'What is Lionel Bromley to you?' he demanded with an abrupt change of subject.

'He has asked me to marry him,' Bella answered honestly.

'I forbid it!'

'*You* forbid it—?'

'As your kinsman, as head of the family, I refuse to allow such a marriage!' he said harshly. His eyes were ablaze with raw, possessive passion.

'Oh, Resaldar . . .' Helplessly she shook her head. And then, without meaning to, she heard herself bursting out, 'It's not too late—it's not as if you were married to Fawzia! I'm quite sure it would be a relief to her if you ended the engagement, because she does not love you, and it would mean that she would not have to sacrifice her religion—'

'Arabella.' The formal use of her full name added to the sombreness of his tone. 'You don't understand. Whatever happens, I must marry Fawzia. There is no way out.'

'No, I don't understand,' Bella whispered with pain.

He lifted his hand, and touched her hair. 'It is not the way an engagement presumably is in your country. If I were to reject her, after she has been at Shapoora under my protection for so long, it would be the greatest degradation I could possibly heap upon her. No one else would marry her, and she would be regarded as an object of shame by her father and her tribe. At worst her father would have her murdered; at best he would keep her locked away, an outcast, so that she would not continue to remind him of his shame. How could I possibly condemn her to that?'

'But—if you were to give up your ambition to become the Emir of Kabul, then her father—'

'It would make no difference,' he cut her short. 'If I were to become the most degenerate of nomads, I would still have to marry her, and she would still have to join her lot with mine.'

'There—really is no way . . .' Bella muttered through numb lips.

'No way at all,' he confirmed bleakly. He seemed about to add something, and then changed his mind and left abruptly.

Life at Shapoora seemed more unendurable than ever to Bella after that night. In an obscure way, it would have helped if she had been able to resent and dislike Fawzia. But the girl was so detached and self-effacing, so negative almost, that it was impossible to harbour strong feelings towards her. Fawzia neither felt passion nor inspired it. And Bella, remembering the passion of which Resaldar was capable, knew that his marriage would be a cold and lonely hell, no matter how hard Fawzia might try to serve him and live only for him. The knowledge brought no comfort at all.

The village was thrown into a ferment of excitement when Flynn finally returned from Gandamak. That evening the three girls stood at the loopholes, watching the feasting which took place around the fire in the courtyard. Once more the tribesmen danced, their swords flashing in the firelight, spinning together with such precision that no matter how close the drawn swords appeared to come to neighbouring limbs, no mishaps occurred.

The three girls had to wait until the morning before they learnt the news which Flynn had brought back. Resaldar called at the house, and told them the decision.

'Major Cavagnari is to hold a *Durbar*, or conference meeting, with those tribal chiefs who have signalled their willingness to accept British intervention in the affairs of Afghanistan. I am to arrive in time for the *Durbar*, to be presented to the chiefs as their future Emir. We shall therefore be leaving for Gandamak in the morning.'

'And not before time!' Nicolette cried, and added, 'I absolutely refuse to travel on a camel!'

Resaldar glanced at her with amusement. 'No, we shall be using horses.' He turned to Fawzia, and addressed her with the formality with which they always treated one another.

'You will accompany us, Highness. If you are to convert, then I wish to ask one of the Army chaplains to instruct you in the Catechism.'

'Very well, my lord Khan.'

During the remainder of the day the village was thrown into a fever of activity. Camels had to be loaded with food supplies, with swords, lances and flint-lock pistols. The small, powerful Waziri horses were driven in from grazing and freshly shod for the journey. Resaldar, Flynn and Fawzia, together with the four hostages, were to travel by horseback; the servants and provisions would accompany them on camels.

Bella went to bed that night, conscious of the fact that it was the last one she would ever spend at Shapoora, and that tomorrow she would be taking the first step towards the final and inevitable parting with Resaldar. When they reached Gandamak she would ask the Army for an escort to the railhead for herself and Simon. And somehow, in the interval, she would have to tell Lionel Bromley that she could not marry him. Once, before she had experienced love, she might have been content with second best. But not any longer.

The village stirred to life long before dawn the next morning. In the grey, unreal light, the camels began to leave Shapoora in procession. Bella shivered with cold, and heaved herself easily into the saddle of her little horse. Nicolette, she noticed, was being helped by Flynn with exaggerated gallantry, and Fawzia looked ghostlike as she sat, side-saddle, upon her horse, draped in *chador* and veil and flanked by two servants mounted on camels.

Resaldar picked up his reins and signalled a command to the others to follow him out of the village. And at that moment everything was plunged into hellish confusion as gunshots mingled with the high-pitched screams of the camels which had just left Shapoora.

It took Bella an instant to realise what was happening. The village had been ambushed by enemies who had chosen their moment with devilish cunning. They must have been lying silently in wait throughout the night.

The tribesmen of Shapoora surged forward to defend their village, and to prevent their camels with their precious loads from falling into enemy hands.

Resaldar, after the first frozen moment of surprise, was preparing to scramble from the saddle to assume command of the defence.

Bella heard Nicolette scream, and then her own blood seemed to freeze in her veins. A man of nightmarishly villainous appearance had somehow slipped through the defence and now loomed before them out of the grey morning light.

His full beard had been dyed a bright, menacing red, and his eyebrows and lashes had been painted black. His expression was one of fanaticism, of barely controlled savagery. The morning light glinted dully on the blade of the knife in his hand.

Resaldar, who had drawn his pistol, hesitated for some inexplicable reason. And in that moment the knife hurtled through the air and found its target, and Resaldar made a groaning sound as he slumped sideways in the saddle, the knife embedded obscenely in his chest.

CHAPTER
SIX

FOR AN INSTANT the mounted party inside Shapoora's walls remained frozen like a tableau, mesmerised with horror. Flynn was the first to react. He drew his pistol and fired at the red-bearded man, who slumped to the ground. Furious fighting was taking place around the gateway into Shapoora, and it did not seem as if the tribesmen would be able to hold off the invaders for much longer.

'Let's get out of here!' Flynn shouted. 'Follow me; there's another concealed exit!'

As if in a trance Fawzia, Nicolette and Lionel began to obey. But, ignoring the Irishman, Bella scrambled from her horse and ran to where Resaldar sprawled in the saddle, and a moment later she was joined by Simon.

'Leave him!' Flynn bellowed over his shoulder at them. ''Tis too late to help him!'

'Bella, for the love of heaven, there's nothing you can do!' Lionel implored. 'He looks to be mortally wounded—'

She scarcely heard them. She touched Resaldar's shoulder and, as she did so, his eyes opened and gazed into hers, clouded with pain but fully aware of the situation.

'Leave me,' he whispered, echoing Flynn's advice. 'Save yourself . . .'

She shook her head. With her teeth grimly set, and

struggling against a feeling of sickness, she began to ease the knife from the wound while Simon held Resaldar's body as still as possible.

Mercifully, he had not fallen forward in such a way as to drive the knife in even further. Its path had been deflected by the bandolier which he wore across his chest, so that it had entered at an angle and thus, Bella prayed devoutly, missed any vital organ. But blood began to spurt from the wound with renewed force, and Resaldar had lost consciousness again.

The enemy were gaining against the desperate tribesmen of Shapoora. 'Bejasus, woman!' Flynn yelled. 'Yer endangerin' us all! Himself is after dying anyway! Save yerself and yer brother and get out!' He leant from the saddle and cracked his whip at the nervous cluster of horses, and they fled with their riders in a clatter of hoofs.

'Bella,' Simon said urgently, 'we'll have to get Resaldar out of here right away!'

The enemy were beginning to surge inside the walls of Shapoora now. The alternatives which faced Bella and Simon were grim. If they moved Resaldar without trying to stanch the bleeding first, he might well die. But unless they fled with him immediately all three of them would be killed.

The most Bella could do was to push her folded handkerchief against the wound underneath Resaldar's tunic. 'I'm lighter than you,' she told her brother as she scrambled into the saddle behind Resaldar. 'You follow Flynn, and try and take my horse with you if you can catch him.'

Simon nodded and ran to where the two riderless horses were cowering nervously. He hurled himself back into the saddle, grabbing the reins of Bella's mount in his free hand. She followed with Resaldar, zigzagging through the village in the direction Flynn had taken. She could only pray that she or Simon would be able to find the concealed exit in time.

Fortunately Flynn and his party had left open the second door after escaping through it, and they could see it clearly as they skirted the harem. Bella urged Simon to dismount and close it behind them, deeming it worth the sacrifice of a few seconds. The door had been designed to fit flush with the wall surrounding Shapoora, and had been skilfully rendered over with mud on both sides so that it accurately matched the wall in appearance.

Away in the distance, etched against the desolate scree, she could see the moving figures of the others on their horses. From behind came the savage sounds of battle as the villagers of Shapoora resisted their attackers and prepared to hold out to the end.

A little way to the east, Bella could see a clump of tamarisk trees, and she gestured to Simon to head for their protective cover. It seemed like a miracle when they reached it to find that the trees grew on the bank of a stream.

Bella helped Simon to lift the unconscious Resaldar from the saddle. He had lost a great deal of blood, and his face was ominously pale and drawn, his lashes very dark against his cheeks, giving him a hauntingly youthful look.

With strips torn from her petticoat, she cleaned the wound. The water in the stream was bitterly cold, for it had flowed from the regions of snow and ice high up in the mountains. The extreme cold of the water had the effect of stanching the bleeding to quite a dramatic degree. Bella used more strips of cloth, wrung out in the water, to plug the wound.

The sun had appeared, bathing the landscape in sharp light and shadows. Bella looked up from her task to find that Flynn and his party, who had earlier been starkly silhouetted against the distant eroded cliffs, were no longer in sight.

'Simon,' she addressed her brother with a worried frown. 'You'd better leave me here and go quickly after Flynn. Persuade them to wait, and ask Lionel to come back and help me with Resaldar.'

He nodded, and mounted his horse, and galloped away. Bella looked at Resaldar with dread in her heart. Had he lost too much blood to survive?

She touched his pale lips with her own, as if to breathe life into him. His eyes flickered open and looked into hers.

The sounds of fighting from Shapoora could easily be heard. Resaldar said with difficulty, 'Take your horse—and go. You must not—be found with me.'

'I'm staying,' she returned quietly.

'Arabella—*Cousin* . . .' His voice was harsh with urgency. 'That man—with the dyed beard . . . He was my great-uncle Wali Mahomed. He—and the other claimants—want to kill me—before I can be proclaimed Emir. So you must leave me—to take my chances—'

Spent by the effort he had made, he drifted into unconsciousness once more. Even in spite of his confirmation that the attack on Shapoora had not been a chance or a random one, but a planned attempt to kill its Khan, Bella felt a little cheered by the fact that Resaldar had gained consciousness, even briefly.

A little later, Simon returned. 'Lionel and I,' he told Bella grimly, 'decided that I had better be the one to come back. That rat, Flynn, would have ridden rough-shod over me and would not have waited. Lionel is making sure that he does.'

Bella cast an anxious look at Resaldar. 'Is the track very rough?'

'It's not too bad. They have found a kind of natural amphitheatre where there is water, and mulberry trees, and even caves in the hills in which to shelter. We shall be able to rest up there while Resaldar recovers.'

Between them, Simon and Bella manoeuvred Resaldar's unconsious body into the saddle. They removed his silk head-dress and used it to strap him into place upon the horse. Then, with Simon holding on to its reins with his free hand, the three little Waziri horses followed the track which Flynn had taken.

It wound ever upwards, bleak and desolate, the earth red and burning hot now as the sun gained in strength. Dust swirled about like a malevolent sienna-coloured cloud. They passed close by some Pathan nomads encamped in black goatskin tents, who paid them no attention once it became obvious that the travellers had no designs on their sheep grazing on the mountain slope.

At last they reached the spot where Flynn and the others were waiting. A flat, circular expanse of green grass shaded by mulberry trees, it was bounded by the cliffs with their jagged overhanging outcrops of rock so that it did, indeed, give the impression of an amphitheatre. At one end of the cliffs a waterfall hurled down to a spring at its foot. It was a strangely tranquil, idyllic scene in the midst of so much desolation.

Lionel hurried forward to meet them, and helped Bella to dismount. He held on to her hand afterwards. 'I have been utterly distraught with anxiety!' he told her. 'Flynn threatened to shoot me if I attempted to go back into the village for you. He was concerned, of course, that I might lead the enemy to himself!'

Bella brushed the explanation aside. 'Please help Simon to lift Resaldar down.'

Flynn himself appeared at the mouth of one of the caves, his arm about Nicolette, who appeared to have been weeping. He left her there and approached Bella.

'Will himself live, d'ye suppose?'

She looked grimly at him. The question had not been asked out of concern. There was no loyalty in Flynn, no feelings of compassion for a stricken friend and benefactor. He was attempting to reassess his own position. If Resaldar was in danger of dying, then Flynn would have to decide where else his own best interests lay.

'Resaldar will live,' she said, her fingers tightly crossed behind her back.

'The Holy Mother be praised,' Flynn said in an unctuous voice.

Lionel and Simon were carrying Resaldar inside one of the caves, and Bella followed. The cave, she discovered, was more than a mere hollow carved out of the rock by time and erosion.

The roof had been vaulted and the walls carefully rendered with what looked like cement. The floor was perfectly level, and the cave itself was wide and spacious extending through the solid rock of the hill for some forty feet.

Bella found Fawzia by her side as she knelt to examine the wound. 'I have made a poultice of wild herbs,' Fawzia said, 'which will protect against infection. It is an old remedy.'

Bella moved aside so that Fawzia could apply the poultice to the wound, painfully reminded that if anyone had the right to concern herself with nursing Resaldar it was Fawzia.

After his wound had been bound up again, the two girls remained seated by his unconscious form. 'The cave will protect him from the heat of the sun,' Fawzia remarked. 'It is fortunate that we found this place.'

Bella glanced about her. 'The caves were not naturally formed, were they?'

'They were excavated by Buddhists, very many years ago, who used them as hermit cells,' Fawzia explained.

Resaldar had been born in a Buddhist cave, Bella remembered. *It had sheltered his mother and father after they fled from Kabul. Was he*, she wondered with fear clutching at her heart, *fated to die in a similar cave?*

She would not allow the thought to take root. 'We shall have to stay here until Resaldar has fully recovered.'

The others had entered the cave too, and had heard her last words. 'We owe him nothing!' Nicolette cried vengefully. 'After all, he had us kidnapped in the first place! So let us leave him here, and make our way to Gandamak without him!'

'Whisht, darlin',' Flynn soothed. 'Whatever yer feelins might be about himself, 'tis to our advantage to wait a few days before we go on. The marauders who attacked Shapoora will be safely out of the way by then.' He added thoughtfully, ''Tis a wonder to me how they came to choose their moment so well, and why the Khan did not shoot that red-bearded spalpeen when he had the chance . . .'

Bella said nothing. If Flynn knew that it was Resaldar's own great-uncle who had come to kill him, he would also know that the attack had been sparked off when Wali Mahomed received instructions to attend a *Durbar* for the purpose of meeting the new Emir-elect. And Flynn would therefore realise that Wali Mahomed was not likely to be the only one of the other claimants to the throne who would have conceived the notion of going to Shapoora to ambush and kill Resaldar. In those circumstances, would the Irishman, who always put his own interests first, scruple to abandon the man who was being sought by so many would-be assassins?

Oh, Resaldar, Bella thought with anguish, *why could*

you not have put aside your commitment to Afghanistan, and settled for your inheritance of Haverington Hall and safety instead?

'We couldn't stay here for days!' Nicolette exclaimed. 'We would starve to death—'

'No, *mavourneen*, we would not,' Flynn assured her. 'We could live well enough on mulberries for a day or two. After that it should be safe for some of us to return to Shapoora and collect more supplies.'

Bella rose abruptly and left the cave. The sun was beating remorselessly down, the enclosing cliffs reflecting and intensifying the heat, so that even the horses had sought shelter inside one of the other caves. The air was filled with the pungent smell of fallen mulberries fermenting in the sun.

Could she, Bella was arguing with herself, *allow Flynn or anyone else to return to Shapoora for supplies, knowing that the village would probably be overrun with the conjoined forces of all of Resaldar's enemies?*

A shadow fell across her, and she realised that Lionel had come to join her. 'My dear Bella,' he said, 'your action this morning fills me with the deepest admiration. Simon is young and impulsive and he acts without thinking. But *you*—you must have known exactly how dangerous it would be to stay behind so that you could help your cousin. A cousin, I might add, who has done nothing to deserve such family loyalty—'

'Lionel,' she interrupted quietly, 'I was not being brave, and it was not done out of family loyalty. I love Resaldar. If he dies, I shouldn't wish to live.'

He was silent for a long while. 'And he—?'

'He must marry Fawzia,' Bella said tonelessly.

'My dear.' He laid his arm gently across her shoulder. 'I do not cut a romantic figure, such as he does. I do not aspire to any great heights, and my aims and ambitions are modest. I can offer you only such solid qualities as loyalty and support and the greatest affection. They are there, if you should ever consent to accept second best.'

'Oh, Lionel . . .' Her eyes filled with tears. 'You are a truly good and generous man . . .'

He gave her a wry smile. 'Not so good or generous that I am not filled with jealousy towards your cousin, the Khan. Come, my dear Bella,' he changed the subject. 'Let us get out of this heat before we develop sunstroke.'

Inside the cave, the hours passed slowly. Resaldar appeared to have fallen into a natural sleep, and the rest of them sat around, making desultory conversation.

Even Nicolette deigned, for the first time, to explain her reasons for being in Afghanistan, although it was primarily to Flynn that she addressed herself. What she left out, Bella was able to read between the lines.

The only child of wealthy, doting parents, Nicolette had never come up against adversity or sorrow until her mother died when the girl was fifteen. But to compensate her for her loss, General Prewitt had made his daughter his whole world. There was no whim of hers which he refused to indulge.

Some eighteen months ago, however, her nose had been put severely out of joint when her father remarried. '*That woman*' was how Nicolette referred venomously to her stepmother.

'She wished to dictate my life,' Nicolette confided to Flynn. 'She claimed to be too delicate to follow Papa to Afghanistan, and I was forced to remain in London with her. To begin with, I agreed. But that woman claimed the right to question my clothes, my friends, the social activities I should or should not take part in . . .'

'To be sure, but she sounds a dragon,' Flynn commiserated.

'We had the most fearful quarrel, and I decided to join

Papa. When it came to it, that woman was too lily-livered to stop me!'

Her stepmother, Bella thought privately, had probably been hugely relieved to be rid of the spoilt, headstrong girl.

'If I had known,' Nicolette added, becoming tearful, 'that I would be kidnapped by savages, and then forced to starve in a cave, I would have put up with that woman's domineering ways instead!'

'Ah, me lovely, but I should not then have had the pleasure of meetin' you,' Flynn murmured, his eyes appraising her, and Nicolette's tears melted into a coquettish smile.

The flirtation between them, Bella thought cynically, would last only until they reached Gandamak, for General Prewitt had a very low opinion of the Irishman and would soon stamp hard upon any incipient relationship between him and Nicolette.

When the last of the sun was drenching the landscape with a golden light, and the temperature had dropped, they left the cave to gather mulberries. After that unsatisfying meal they huddled close together inside the cave for warmth and tried to sleep.

The next morning Resaldar's wound looked clean and healthy, but his face was haggard and his eyes deeply shadowed. The loss of so much blood had weakened him dangerously, and Bella knew that unless he received more nourishment than could be obtained from mulberries, he would be prey to all kinds of infections and might even develop gangrene.

Struck by a sudden inspiration and an accompanying spasm of fear, she turned to Flynn. 'There are Pathan nomads encamped not far from here, herding their sheep. Are they likely to—well, to inform any of Shapoora's enemies that they saw us coming this way?'

'They will not. Pathan nomads keep themselves to themselves.'

'And are they likely to present a threat to us in themselves?'

Flynn shook his head. 'They'll not trouble us if we don't trouble them.'

'In that case,' Bella said, picking up the length of blue silk which had formed Resaldar's headdress. 'Will you offer this to them in exchange for such food as they can provide?'

The Irishman nodded thoughtfully, and left on his errand. When he returned later he was accompanied by two of the Pathans carrying earthenware pots containing boiled ewes' milk, some loaves of freshly baked bread and a goatskin filled with curd-like cheese.

Bella insisted that the food should be rationed in such a way that the milk, stored underneath the ice-cold waterfall, and a large share of the cheese would be reserved for Resaldar. Only Nicolette quarrelled with this arrangement.

Resaldar continued to make good progress. A few times during the following days his temperature rose and then subsided again dramatically, but his wound appeared to be healing well.

One evening, when Resaldar's mysterious fever had abated again and he seemed to be sleeping normally, Flynn said, 'I think 'tis time I rode back to Shapoora. We must have camels and armed guides and food supplies if we are to make the journey to Gandamak. The devil of it is that we can't get a glimpse of Shapoora from here, but things should surely have returned to normal in the village by now.'

Bella said nothing, but she lay awake for most of the night, struggling with the dilemma facing her. Should she warn Flynn that the attack on Shapoora had not simply been a random one? That other claimants to the Afghan throne might have set out for Shapoora to make sure that Resaldar never reached Gandamak?

On the other hand, she told herself, there was no real proof that Wali Mahomed, Resaldar's great-uncle, had not acted alone on some mad impulse. The man had certainly looked half-crazed, with his dyed eyebrows and his satanic henna-red beard and his air of fanaticism. And it was true that if they were to reach Gandamak at all they *would* need food supplies and arms from Shapoora . . .

She fell asleep with her dilemma still unsolved, and in the morning the decision had been taken out of her hands, for they awakened to find that their horses had disappeared.

It was improbable that the animals could all have taken it into their heads to leave the warmth and shelter of their cave and stray. Flynn, Lionel and Simon set out to search for signs of them.

Flynn was the first to return, and grimly he reported that the Pathan nomads had struck their tents, gathered up their sheep and departed. The inference was only too obvious. The Pathans might not offer violence, or interfere in the quarrels of others, but they were no more averse to robbery than any of the other tribes of Afghanistan. Before they left, they had crept up to the caves and stolen the Waziri horses.

Nicolette began to weep with fear and despair. Resaldar, whose temperature was stable this morning, struggled to a sitting position, and said, 'We shall have to walk to Gandamak.'

'I'll do nothing of the sort!' Nicolette cried wildly. 'It's your fault that all this has happened! Savage! Bandit! *Renegade!*'

Flynn tried to calm her, and when she began to

sob hysterically he gave up the attempt and turned to Resaldar.

''Twould be more sensible, surely for us to walk to Shapoora instead, Highness, and re-equip ourselves there for the journey to Gandamak—'

'No,' Resaldar interrupted in a quiet voice. 'We shall have to keep well away from Shapoora, and from the Pass.'

Bella listened numbly as he spelled out what she had been trying to keep from the others.

'Have you not realised, Flynn, what lay behind that attack? It was not mounted by some other mountain tribe for the usual reasons of revenge or gain. My great-uncle Wali Mahomed himself led that attack. The other claimants to the throne will be no less determined to ensure that I do not reach Gandamak to be proclaimed Emir of Kabul.'

'Are you sayin',' Flynn asked slowly, 'that all the claimants sank their differences and banded together to have you killed, Highness?'

'I believe so yes. Wali Mahomed commanded the raid on Shapoora. I am morally certain that, stationed all along the route as far as Gandamak, others will be waiting—supporters of my cousins Hamid Khan and Achmed Isa, not to mention my uncle Yakoob Khan and other lesser kin—to cut off any hope I might have of escaping assassination.'

'And they'll not leave witnesses to tell the tale,' Flynn mused.

'Precisely. Anyone travelling with me would share my fate. So it will be necessary to take a roundabout route through the mountains to Gandamak—'

They were interrupted by the high-pitched scream of a camel coming from close by. Nicolette, shocked out of her hysteria, began to whimper with terror at the sound. But then Simon's eager, excited voice reached them.

'Come and see what Lionel and I have found!'

The camel was one of those from Shapoora which had been packed up with supplies and had already passed through the gate of the village when the attack started. The terrified beast had obviously taken to its heels, and escaped in the confusion.

'We were searching for the horses,' Simon related, 'when Lionel and I caught sight of it inside a gorge. We could see that its load was still intact.'

'But where *is* Lionel?' Bella asked.

'He slipped when we went down into the gorge, and hurt his ankle. I left him limping along behind.'

They were unloading the camel, later, when Lionel arrived. His face was twisted with pain and when he removed his boot it became obvious tht he had sprained his ankle. Bella wrung a cloth out in cold water and gave it to him to apply to the joint, and then walked to where the others were examining the camel's load. Resaldar, using the minimum of movement in order not to re-open his wound, was evaluating the load. He expressed disappointment that there were no firearms or other weapons, for apart from Flynn's pistol they were completely without any means of defence. But among the camel's load were hide containers filled with dried apricots, with nuts and cheese and rock salt for use in cases of dehydration. There were also prayer-rugs which could be used as blankets.

Resaldar said soberly, 'We must not waste the advantage this find gives us. With care, the food could last for a little longer than it would take to walk to Gandamak. But an immediate start will have to be made—'

'I'm going nowhere with you!' Nicolette cried shrilly. 'You said, yourself, that all your relatives are prepared to kill you on sight! You cannot expect us to share your danger!'

'No,' Resaldar agreed quietly. 'That had occurred to me, too. So what I intend to do is this. I shall leave most of the food with you, and take only such provisions as I cannot do without, and make for Gandamak alone. I shall ask the British to send troops immediately to come and escort you to safety.'

'That would be madness!' Bella exclaimed. 'It is only a matter of days since you were wounded. Someone else will have to go!'

'Of course *he* must go!' Nicolette said feverishly. 'As soon as possible. For myself, I don't intend to set foot out of this place until the British Army come to rescue us!'

'Resaldar cannot go alone,' Bella maintained with dogged persistence. 'Apart from anything else, his temperature is unstable. There is no knowing what he might do in the delirium of a high fever.'

Simon cried eagerly, '*I* shall go with him!'

'No!' Resaldar and Bella spoke simultaneously.

Lionel gave a wry grin. 'I would gladly volunteer, but it would be a case of the halt and the lame . . .'

'You could not travel through the mountains with a sprained ankle,' Resaldar agreed. 'And Flynn must stay to protect you all. So there is nothing for it but to go alone.'

'Tell me, Resaldar,' Bella challenged, 'would you be able to take the camel with you?'

'For a short distance only, until the terrain becomes more rugged—'

'And how,' she demanded, 'would you then be able to carry your supplies? Strapped to your back? It would almost certainly cause your wound to re-open. You cannot possibly go alone. I shall go with you.'

'*No!*' he said violently. 'I forbid it!'

'You cannot stop me,' she told him calmly.

His eyes darkened with a mixture of emotions of which anger seemed to be only a small part, and there was something deliberately calculated to wound as he said, 'Even with all my handicaps I should be better off without an encumbrance like you! You'd be more of a hindrance than a help, and I do not want you!'

'Nevertheless,' Bella said quietly, 'I am going. I shall get ready now.'

She was filling one of the goatskins with water for the journey when Lionel limped up to her. 'I cannot like the thought of your accompanying your cousin—'

'The safety of all of us,' Bella interrupted, 'depends on Resaldar reaching Gandamak. His chances would be slim if he set out alone, with no one to nurse him through his fevers, with no one to help him carry the supplies. And who else is there? Simon is only a schoolboy, Fawzia's taboos would forbid her, and Nicolette would not dream of volunteering.'

'At least take Simon with you, for the sake of your reputation—'

'My reputation,' Bella said quietly, 'is worth little when weighed against Simon's safety. He would be far safer staying here where Flynn, for the sake of his own ambitions, will take good care of the hostages.'

Resaldar was in a smouldering mood when they left immediately after the camel had been loaded. It was very much in Bella's mind, as she said goodbye to Simon and the others, that she might never see any of them again.

Following the camel, she and Resaldar thrust further into the mountains, travelling along a narrow gorge. The heat of the sun was made bearable only by the fact that the gorge acted like a funnel through which a cooling breeze blew. High above them rose a range of jagged snow peaks, shimmering in the sun.

They kept going grimly, without speaking. Bella's muscles seemed to be on fire, and she could only guess at the pain and discomfort which Resaldar was experiencing, for he never faltered.

The gorge suddenly opened out into a valley where the mountains were no longer sheer. It was a desolate place, a wilderness where nothing grew and where the earth consisted of pulverised rock. All the winds of Asia seemed to howl over it, and the sun was lost in clouds of dust.

At last, when Bella felt that she had reached the very limit of her endurance, they came upon a ruined and deserted caravanserai, and Resaldar announced tersely that they would make camp there for the night.

They ate their rations in silence, and afterwards Resaldar carried his rug to a corner of the ruin and wrapped himself in it, and settled down to sleep. Bella followed suit, choosing an opposite corner.

She was just drifting into sleep when she became aware that Resaldar's fever had returned. She rose, and moonlight sifting through the holes in the ruined walls marked her way as she hurried to Resaldar. He was shivering and delirious, and unaware of her. She fumbled in the dark for the water, and sponged his face, and then there was nothing else she could do but lie down beside him and try to bring some warmth to his fever-chilled body with her own. She fell asleep from sheer exhaustion, her arm flung about him.

She awakened suddenly, to find that the morning sun was striking gold from Resaldar's tawny hair. His eyes were open and very blue and free of fever, staring into hers.

He moved, suddenly, and his mouth sought hers with

a violence of passion and despair and desire which denied the angry resentment with which he had suffered her company through the mountains.

Her hands moved in the intuitive patterns of love, her flattened palms sliding beneath his tunic, feeling the warmth of his skin beneath her fingers. He caught her to him, raising himself slightly, and his hands began to fumble with desperate urgency at the fastenings of her blouse. She felt his mouth at her throat, travelling to the hollow between her breasts.

Then she was pressed against him, their naked flesh touching, and the hardness of his body sent a tingling surge of feeling to her stomach. Her skirt had been pulled up to her waist and his hands were exploring and caressing her thighs, stroking and moulding and fingering so that she cried out in involuntary encouragement.

Instead, the sound which had escaped her seemed to bring him to his senses. Quite abruptly, he pulled away from her, and with a sense of shame and rejection she began to straighten her clothing.

He sat up, away from her so that they would not touch. His knees were drawn up to his chin, his head sunk into his hands. After a long moment he looked up at her.

'I knew it would be a torment if you came with me,' he said tonelessly. 'And I was right.'

She was still shaken by her own primitive desires, although the sense of rejection had left her, for she knew well enough why he had drawn away.

'Resaldar,' she whispered, 'is there really no way out? *No way at all?*'

'There is a way.' He uttered a laugh which was completely devoid of humour or mirth. 'But I doubt if you would be prepared to take it.'

'I'd do *anything*—' she began.

'Would you?' He caught her wrist in his hand. 'The only possible way, Arabella, would mean denying your creed, your faith and your culture.'

'I don't understand—'

'If you and I were both to convert to Islam, I would not have to make a choice.'

'Convert to Islam?' she echoed in a dazed voice. 'What difference would that—'

'It would,' he answered her half-formed question flatly, 'mean that I could then marry both Fawzia *and* yourself.'

CHAPTER
SEVEN

FOR A FULL minute Bella stared at Resaldar without comprehension. Then, as the meaning of what he had said struck home, she cried with revulsion, 'Dear God— *no*!'

'You said you would do anything—'

'But not *this*, Resaldar!'

His grip on her wrist tightened. 'I realise that the notion is an alien one to you—'

'It is not only alien! It's utterly repugnant, barbaric!'

Resaldar's eyes darkened until they resembled the slate-blue colour of storm-clouds. 'It is something my countrymen accept as normal,' he reminded her.

'Well, *they* are—'

'Barbaric?' he supplied the word, his voice cold and hard now.

'I didn't say that—'

'No, but that is what you meant.' He rose, and stood looking down at her. 'Let us examine the British way for a moment. It is not considered civilised to have more than one wife, so you would have me choose between sending you away, or abandoning Fawzia. Either choice would lead to great unhappiness, even to tragedy if I were to cast Fawzia off. And you think that is less barbaric than what I am suggesting?'

Bella sprang to her feet. 'Resaldar, I can hardly believe that you are serious—'

'No, I can see that.' He took her by the shoulders and pulled her towards him, without passion or desire this time, but merely to make her aware of his brute strength. 'I think you have been making the mistake of seeing me as an Englishman, Cousin Arabella, who just happens to have some Afghan blood in his veins. And because that Afghan blood chances to be royal, you somehow imagine it to be different, superior in some way, more civilised. Well, I am fully as barbaric as my countrymen.'

She said unsteadily, 'If you—continue to hold me in such a—painful way—I shall begin to believe you—'

'You had better believe me.' His hold on her did not relax. 'And there is something else which you should bear in mind. *You* insisted on coming on this expedition with me. Be very careful in future not to goad or tempt me into displaying the full extent of my Afghan barbarism.'

He flung her from him and strode away to look for the camel. Shaken, Bella left the ruined caravanserai too and made her way to where a stream flowed sluggishly over stones. As she washed, her mind examined the scene which had just taken place.

She had not taken Resaldar seriously at first. She had thought that he was merely using bitter irony to illustrate the hopelessness of their situation. But he *had* been serious, and her reaction had angered and insulted him.

For the first time, she considered his suggestion with the same seriousness with which he had offered it. *Could* she possibly overcome her prejudice and agree to it?

On the one hand, she loved him with a possessive, jealous passion which would make sharing him with Fawzia nothing short of torture. But on the other, if she did not share him, she would have nothing. And hadn't her whole life, so far, been one of compromise, of making the best of things?

Sacrificing her faith to embrace another would not be, for Bella, the moral torment which it was to Fawzia. Bella happened to believe that it did not much matter which faith one observed so long as certain principles and tenets were adhered to. She did not believe that the Deity cared whether one addressed Him as God, or Allah, or whatever, provided that one approached life with humility and charity and compassion towards others.

So, if she were to convert to Islam and Resaldar married both herself and Fawzia, she would share the harem at the Emir's Palace in Kabul with the other girl, just as millions of Resaldar's female subjects would be sharing *their* husbands—

She shook her head slowly. She had been overlooking two very important points, and so had Resaldar.

He had once told her, with passion, about his dream of religious tolerance in Afghanistan. He hoped that the fact of his Christianity might help to bring it about. How could she allow him to abandon that dream now by converting to Islam, merely so that they could marry?'

There was another consideration to which neither of them had given any thought. The tribes of Afghanistan would never accept his marriage to an Englishwoman.

It was one thing to ask them to accept a half-English Emir. But he, after all, was the son of their Princess Shazeen; he had been born in Afghanistan and owed no allegiance whatsoever to the country of his father. And he could no more have helped who his father was than he could have helped being baptised into the Christian faith by his parents.

But to ask the Afghans to tolerate a full-blooded Englishwoman as one of his wives . . . That was an altogether different matter. To foist on to them a woman who had been born and bred in the country of their enemies, the hated White Kaffirs, whom they believed had been trying for years to enslave them, would create an explosive situation. It would rock the throne of Kabul to its foundations.

As Bella walked slowly back to the ruins of the caravanserai she reflected that it would be as well to keep a barrier of anger and misunderstanding erected between herself and Resaldar. Without it, thrown together on this expedition as they were, they would be too vulnerable. And the situation was truly hopeless, even if Resaldar did not realise it.

Without any further communication between them, they set out once more after they had breakfasted, following the camel through a rocky defile.

The days became a blur of fatigue and grim endurance. The defile opened up into a broad, shallow valley spread with tawny cliffs upon which the sun glared down without pity. A wind suddenly sprang up, but brought no relief from the heat. It blew dust into their faces and all but blinded them.

'The *Bād-i-Sad-o-Bist*,' Resaldar explained tersely. 'The Wind of a Hundred and Twenty Days.'

Bella hoped devoutly that long before the wind had blown out its allotted span they would have reached their destination. Nothing had prepared her for the sheer awfulness of the expedition.

Resaldar had suffered no recurrence of the fever, and her own rôle was now meaningless. She thought of her brother and the others, who had nothing more unpleasant than boredom to contend with back in their amphitheatre in the hills, and could not help wishing herself back with them. Sometimes, when she caught Resaldar's gaze upon her, the angry glitter of his eyes told her that he, too, was wishing that she had not come.

As they struggled along against the wind it sometimes seemed to Bella that she and Resaldar were the only two people left alive in a barren and desolate world. There was no sign of human occupation anywhere in that mountainous region. The very landscape itself seemed to defy man to colonise it. Umber cliffs and mountains sheer and high as a prison wall; great gorges on which the sun baked down, with only an occasional stunted tamarisk to offer some inadequate shade to the traveller.

But then, one evening, they stumbled upon evidence of the indomitable spirit of man, in the shape of a ruined minaret. It must have been built in the eleventh or twelfth century.

Who had come to worship here, Bella wondered as she sank thankfully into the shade of a ruined wall. *Tribesmen must once have occupied this desolate place for a minaret to have been justified . . .*

She looked up, her gaze transfixed. Resaldar was unloading the camel and she saw him with a suddenly heightened awareness. The sun glinted on his tawny hair, casting a halo of light around his sun-darkened face. His eyes seemed to have acquired an intensity of colour and everything about him radiated a sensual virility. For an instant, silhouetted against the background of ancient hills and ruined minaret, he appeared to Bella's fancy as some mythical being, half-god, half-satyr.

He had become aware of her intense scrutiny. She flushed, and offered the first explanation she could think of for her interest.

'I was thinking—that is, I was wondering from whom you inherited your colouring. None of the portraits of the ancestors in Haverington Hall shows such blue eyes and dark-gold hair . . .'

There was derision in the smile which he turned to

her. 'Of course, you *would* assume that my civilised British blood would predominate and overshadow the Barbaric Afghan. As a matter of fact, I owe my colouring to my grandmother, Shazeen's mother. She was of mixed French and Nordic and Persian ancestry.'

Gratefully Bella seized the excuse to give the conversation a different turn. 'Your mother must have been beautiful. How sad that her life should have ended like that, as a slave to the Infidels.'

Resaldar came to sit down in the shade. 'My mother was the strong partner in the marriage. Had she been the man, she would have found a way of escaping from the Infidels. My father, alas, simply waited in vain for someone else to rescue us.'

Bella ate her ration of dried apricots and cheese, and thought of Shazeen. Had she considered her love for Jack Haverington worth all the dreadful sacrifices which she had been called on to make? To have been born a princess, and to have been forced to flee from a Royal palace and make her home in a cave, before being captured into slavery . . .

Through it all, Shazeen must have retained her spirit and her pride, for she had communicated those qualities to her son. While Resaldar had obviously been educated in English and other subjects by his father, his mother had taught him about the dynastic blood which flowed in his veins, and that he had as much right as anyone else to claim the throne of Afghanistan one day—

'There is a waterfall not far from here,' Resaldar broke into her thoughts. 'I suggest that we take it in turns to bathe.'

'How do you know about the waterfall?' Bella asked curiously.

He shrugged. 'While the tribesmen of Shapoora lived as nomads, we often travelled this route.'

'I see. Well, if you would like to give me your tunic, I'll wash our clothes before I bathe. They will be dry again in the morning.'

He pulled his dusty tunic over his head and, clad only in his wide-legged pantaloons, left for the waterfall. Bella followed suit a while later, after Resaldar had returned. She bathed and washed her hair under the waterfall and then, with her sleeping rug wrapped round her like a sarong, she returned to the ruin and spread their clothes out on the wall to dry overnight.

Shazeen continued to occupy her thoughts. Resaldar's mother had roamed this track with the nomads whose prisoner she was; she must often have bathed in that same waterfall and washed her clothes . . .

Bella lay down beside one of the broken walls. Moonlight slanted through the gaps in the ruin and touched Resaldar's hair with silver. He lay on his rug with his arms folded behind his head.

'It has always surprised me,' Bella said aloud, 'that Shazeen should have been able to conduct a love affair with Jack Haverington in the first place. He was tutor to her brothers, and with strict segregation of the sexes, there would have been scant opportunity for them to meet at all, let alone in private . . .'

Resaldar turned on his side, and supported himself on one elbow. 'My mother was a woman of passion and spirit and courage. She saw my father, and wanted him. She defied the conventions and the taboos; she ignored the dangers, and took what she wanted.' Bella could almost see that derisive smile curving Resaldar's lips as he added, 'But then, she was not civilised, like you.'

With careful deliberation, Bella got to her feet and allowed the rug to fall on the ground. She went to kneel beside him, her bare skin gleaming silver-gilt in the moonlight, her head flung up in a challenge.

'You have taunted me once too often, Resaldar,' she said softly.

Slowly, as though mesmerised, he sat up and put out his arms. His palms moved on her shoulders, his fingertips exploring the twin wings of her shoulderblades, his hands slightly unsteady as they slid down to the hollow of her back. She moved so that the skin of his naked chest made contact with her own bare flesh in a sensation which was, at once, totally unfamiliar and yet had an element of recognition, of *rightness*, about it.

'Civilised women,' Bella murmured, 'have their share of passion and spirit and courage too, Resaldar.'

He made no reply. His mouth moved on hers, drawing response from her entire being. Just as she felt as though she were drifting down into a bottomless void, he lifted his head. He took hold of a handful of her hair in a gesture which was at once angry and tender.

'Truly,' he said, 'your civilised ways are incomprehensible to me! You were outraged and disgusted at the notion of sharing me with Fawzia in lawful and honourable matrimony. And yet, for what you're offering me now, you could be put to death in my country!'

Sighing, she traced the outline of his mouth with her fingertip. 'Resaldar, the Afghan tribes may well accept you for their Emir as the price of peace with Britain. But they would never accept a British wife into the bargain.'

'They would accept what I dictate—' he began autocratically.

'No. Lionel Bromley has told me something of the history of this country. The British are hated and feared because it is believed that they wish to impose their laws on the people and make slaves of the free hill-tribes. If you were to marry me, can't you understand how the matter would be regarded? The tribes would consider that you had betrayed them, that you had entered into collusion with the enemy.'

When he remained silent, Bella went on, 'I can see you are forced to accept that I am right. So—let us take what little we can, even if I *do* risk being put to death.'

He pulled her close and kissed her lips, very gently. Then he held her away from him.

'You are my true love, Arabella, but you are also my kinswoman.' In the moonlight his eyes had a look of sad and tender amusement. 'And it is one of our barbaric Afghan customs that our kinswomen should be protected at all times—even from themselves.'

He picked up his rug and wrapped it about her, his hands lingering for the briefest of moments. 'Stay here, and go to sleep.'

She watched as he collected her own discarded rug and left the ruin, to find some other sleeping place for himself, and did not know whether to feel glad or sorry that his iron self-control had averted a situation from which there could have been no turning back.

In the morning, neither of them referred to what had happened. Resaldar's manner towards Bella had subtly changed. He had called her his kinswoman, and it was as if he were constantly reminding himself now that she was his younger, female cousin whom he had to guard and protect and rule over with a teasing authority. Bella sensed that this was as much a shield for his true feelings as his earlier taunting anger towards her had been.

'We are going to have to part company with the camel here, Cousin', he mentioned casually after they had breakfasted.

'Why? We have not yet reached hills which are impassable for the beast—'

'We'll be too conspicuous, travelling with the animal. We shall also have to start doing our travelling by night, and hiding by day.'

'Hiding, Resaldar? Who on earth from? There is no sign of life in this desolate landscape—'

He laughed grimly. 'Don't be deceived by appearances. These hills have always been inhabited, and they still are. This is the home of the Koku Khel.'

'Who are they?'

'The most cunning of murderous robbers. They are said to be descended from stragglers in the army of Alexander the Great.'

Bella cast an uneasy glance about her. In the morning light of sharp sunshine and shadows the hills and the distant snow-peaked mountains lay bathed in innocence. The landscape had an untouched quality, not so much of desolation this morning but as of a place undefiled by man. It was difficult to believe that what Resaldar was saying was true.

'The Koku Khel,' he went on, 'have a habit of dropping as swiftly and unexpectedly as vultures on their prey, and afterwards they retreat back into the hills where it is often impossible to follow them.'

'Without the camel,' Bella said nervously, 'we should have nothing worth stealing. We would be safe enough without the camel, wouldn't we?'

'To the Koku Khel *anything* is worth murdering and robbing for. They would kill you for the gown you are wearing, Cousin, and my embroidered tunic would be considered a rare prize by them.' Resaldar frowned. 'I wish we might have been able to choose more subdued clothing. We are much too conspicuous. Yes, I think it would be wise to carry on only until midday, and then turn the camel loose and rest until nightfall.'

The ill-tempered camel gave a high-pitched, derisive

scream as they sent it on its way at noon. They had found a mountain stream in which the water was clear and cold, for it had its source somewhere up in the snowy peaks. They decided to follow the stream until they should come upon some place which afforded shelter in which to rest until nightfall.

Bella suddenly felt Resaldar's hand on her arm, the pressure of his fingers conveying a warning. He drew her down into the inadequate shelter of a berberis shrub and pointed to the horizon.

'Look—a caravan.'

'Are they Koku Khel?' she asked anxiously.

Resaldar shook his head. 'Nomads. It's as well that they shouldn't see us.'

When the convoy of camels came closer, Bella realised that the beasts were being ridden exclusively by women, while the men, armed with ancient flint-locks and murderous-looking knives, sauntered alongside with a carefree and nonchalant air.

The women sat high on corded bales strapped to the backs of the camels, their bodies wrapped in the black folds of their *chadori*. These were not like the garments worn by the women in the harem at Shapoora. They were, instead, all-enveloping bell-like robes which covered the women from head to foot, with what appeared like crocheted holes for the eyes.

In spite of their cumbersome *chadori*, the women controlled their camels with astonishing dexterity. With them on their shifting platforms they carried utensils like copper cauldrons, gourds and bottles made of animal skin for the carrying of water, and even livestock, such as fowls, tied by the leg.

The younger women herded the nomads' sheep, or helped to keep the children in order. In startling contrast with the black ugliness of the women's *chadori*, the camels wore neckbands of exquisite coloured embroidery.

'They are on their way to find summer pasture for their sheep,' Resaldar explained. Then he stiffened with dismay.

The caravan was halting only a few yards away from them, making it impossible for them either to go on or to retreat without being seen. They would have to hide in the cramped shelter of the berberis shrub until the caravan moved on or until night fell.

Bella and Resaldar lay and watched the activities of the nomads. While the men sat in a circle and gossiped, some of the women lit fires and set their cauldrons upon the embers. Other women walked downstream until they were so close that Bella could almost have stretched out a hand and touched the hem of an all-enveloping *chador*. After filling their leather containers with water, the women began to do their laundry. Soon were spread out upon the banks to dry the children's pantaloons and smocks and some dozen or so black *chadori*. Either the men did not possess a change of clothing, or else they considered it unmasculine to have their clothes laundered.

Resaldar was eyeing the spread-out clothing with speculation. In that fierce heat it would not take long before they were dry and then the women would gather them up once more and the caravan would depart. Since the nomads had not pitched their tents, they obviously meant to go on after they had eaten.

The women who had been busy at the campfires announced that the meal was ready, and everyone crowded round. Bella became aware that Resaldar was inching forward very stealthily to where the clothing had been spread out to dry.

He crept back into the shelter of the berberis, two

chadori clutched to his chest. 'Put it on,' he commanded
Bella, handing her one of the garments.

She pulled it over her head without argument. She
understood his reasoning. As two robed, veiled tribes-
women they would be quite anonymous in these hills,
not worthy of the attention of the Koku Khel. She stifled
a giggle at sight of Resaldar, only his blue eyes visible
through the crocheted holes of the *chador*, and then lost
all desire to laugh as he ordered coolly,

'Come, we're going to join them for lunch.'

'You're crazy!' she whispered.

'No, it's the only way. They'll discover the loss of the
chadori as soon as they've eaten, and therefore we can't
go on hiding here. We'll join them, and wander away
afterwards as if wishing to stretch our legs, and by the
time they realise what happened we shall have lost
ourselves in the hills.'

Bella was never to know whether or not they would
have got away with the masquerade, for in the next
instant the scene was transformed into one of unspeakable nightmare.

Resaldar had said that the Koku Khel dropped upon
their prey like vultures, and this was indeed what they
resembled as they hurled themselves out of the hills on
to the nomads. They came on small, fleet black ponies,
their cutlasses blinking in the sun, their pistols cracking
with deadly accuracy. The nomads had no chance at all.
Some of the women fled into the hills with their children,
but those who stayed and tried to help the men to defend
their property were cut down without mercy by the
Koku Khel.

Resaldar had forced Bella flat on the ground underneath the berberis, and they lay still, hardly breathing,
peering through the eye-holes of their *chadori* as the
Koku Khel proceeded to gather up whatever loot they

could find. Nothing, it seemed, was too trivial for their attention; when the nomads' possessions had been packed up on the backs of the camels, someone pointed to the laundry which had been left out to dry, and two men came to collect it. Bella, waiting with her heart in her mouth, sensed the precise moment when she and Resaldar were spotted.

The Koku Khel stood over them, prodding them with the blunt edge of their cutlasses, signalling to them to rise. It soon appeared that they were not to be killed. The Koku Khel had a use for them. They were to herd the nomads' sheep up to the fastness of the robbers.

As they trudged behind the sheep, surrounded by the Koku Khel, Bella whispered with fear and despair, 'What—what will they do with us once we have served our purpose?'

It was a moment before Resaldar answered. 'They will kill me when they discover that I am not a woman. And you—'

'Yes?'

'I wish to God,' he said sombrely, 'that I could believe they would kill you too . . .'

Numbed by fear, Bella stumbled after the sheep. At nightfall there was still no sign of a village being reached, and it began to appear that the Koku Khel had been on their way home from some other nefarious enterprise when they chanced upon the hapless nomads.

By means of gestures, Bella and Resaldar were ordered to light fires and prepare a meal with provisions stolen from the nomads. As their captors were eating, Bella noticed that the man who appeared to be their chief wore an Army medal pinned to his turban. She wondered what had happened to the poor British soldier whose property it had been.

It was clear that there would be no opportunity to

attempt escaping that night, for the Koku Khel took it in turns to keep watch over the camp. Bella and Resaldar lay close together and tried to sleep, and she could not help wondering whether this would be their last night alive.

At dawn they were made to gather the sheep and begin herding them up the mountains once more.

It was not until late in the afternoon that they came within sight of the Koku Khel village. Its houses had been built in the domed, *yurt* shape, the primitive style passed down by the Mongols. They were enclosed in blank walls with a high watch-tower at each corner. But there was a strange air of desolation about the village; no sound of voices rang out, no faces appeared at the watch-towers to see who was approaching. Bella and Resaldar could sense that their captors, too, were struck by the strangely deserted atmosphere of the village.

They were halted there below the village, discussing the situation, when a bugle suddenly sounded. It seemed to come from nowhere and everywhere.

The Koku Khel were clearly unnerved and undecided. The next moment it was too late for them to plan any course of action, for what had seemed no more than the ordinary, familiar crags in the rocks of the surrounding hills suddenly revealed themselves to have been used as hiding places.

Horses whickered and shots rang out as British cavalry, supported by Bengal Lancers, came pouring from their hiding places in an avalanche, to descend upon the Koku Khel who had been caught like rats in a trap.

Even though they were hopelessly outnumbered and had been taken entirely by surprise, the Koku Khel fought with incredible, savage bravery, desperately discharging their flint-locks and rushing in with their cutlasses. But they could not have hoped to withstand the might of the enemy which had been waiting to ambush them. An hour later there was not one survivor, and Bella found the attention of the commanding officer turning to herself and Resaldar, where they had been taking shelter behind a large rock.

'March these two hags to where the other women are being confined,' he ordered some of his men, 'and then set fire to the village.'

Bella flung up her head. 'This particular hag has no intention of being marched anywhere, Captain!'

'Good heavens!' His jaw fell open. 'What—? Who are you?'

Resaldar loomed over her, something in his attitude warning her to tread cautiously. Swiftly he seized the initiative, and answered for her.

'We hoped that by wearing *chadori* we would be inconspicuous,' he told the officer, side-stepping the latter's question. 'However, it did not prevent the Koku Khel from capturing us, and forcing us to herd their sheep.'

Bella stifled a spasm of hysterical laughter at the look of ludicrous disbelief on the face of the officer as he listened to Resaldar's deep male voice issuing from the essentially feminine *chador*.

'Britishers,' the captain muttered. Then, trying to gain authority over the situation, he demanded once more, 'Who *are* you? Damn-fool missionaries, rushing in where angels fear to tread? Or—' his voice deepened with suspicion—'an Army deserter and his light-of-love trying to make for the border?'

Resaldar hesitated for only a fraction of a second before he said, 'We are brother and sister. We came to Afghanistan on a private mission. Soon after we left the Pass we were captured by brigands and held prisoner—'

A look of excitement crossed the captain's features.

'Were you, by any chance, among the poor devils taken hostage by the Khan of Shapoora?'

Bella was wondering, confusedly, why Resaldar did not immediately announce that *he* was the Khan of Shapoora, that the hostages were safe, and that he was on his way to the *Durbar* at Gandamak to be proclaimed Emir of Afghanistan.

Instead, he was saying with careful detachment, 'It's interesting, Captain, that you should mention the Khan of Shapoora. What do you know about him?'

'Principally that he is being hunted by both the British Army and the Afghan tribes.' The captain laughed grimly. 'For his sake, I hope the Army catches up with him first and hangs him in a humane and civilised manner. If they don't—'

He shrugged. 'Well, the Afghans have some pretty nasty ways of disposing of their enemies.'

CHAPTER
EIGHT

TRYING TO contain the flesh-crawling fear which had suddenly taken hold of her, Bella strove desperately to marshal her thoughts into some kind of coherence.

Why would the British be searching for Resaldar *in order to hang him*? They wished to place him on the throne of Afghanistan, and had summoned him to the *Durbar* at Gandamak for that reason . . .

One thing, at least, was becoming clear to her. She was beginning to understand the reason for Resaldar's caution. In Afghanistan one did not survive by taking any individual or any situation on trust.

Her breath caught as a sudden thought occurred to her. Could the Army have been engaged upon a monstrous bluff from the very beginning? Had Major Cavagnari's sole motive been to force Resaldar from the secure fastness of Shapoora and out into the open, where he would be vulnerable?

But no, she argued with herself, General Prewitt would never have gone along with a scheme of that kind. *His* only concern was to get his daughter Nicolette safely restored to him, and Major Cavagnari was his personal friend as well as his fellow-officer. Unless General Prewitt had been callously deceived, too, by Major Cavagnari and General Maude . . .

The British officer opened his mouth to speak again, but Bella forestalled him. 'I—my brother and I—we heard rumours that the Army intended to proclaim the Khan of Shapoora the country's new Emir—'

'Yes, there was some such scheme—'The captain's eyes narrowed with suspicion. 'What is your interest in the Khan of Shapoora? For two private visitors to Afghanistan, you seem to have made it your business to seek out local rumour! I ask you again—just who *are* you?'

Smoothly, Resaldar took charge of the situation once again. 'I am John Haverington,' he said, 'and this is my sister, Arabella.'

It struck Bella with a small shock that the statement was only half a lie. As well as being the Khan of Shapoora, Resaldar was also a Haverington, and his second name must be John, after his father.

'And what is the private mission which brought you to Afghanistan?' the officer demanded.

'My sister is unofficially engaged to a war correspondent named Lionel Bromley,' Resaldar explained glibly. 'When Bromley stopped writing to her she became so low in spirits that I feared for her health. In spite of the dangers involved in entering Afghanistan, I decided that we should come and confront him and put an end to my sister's state of uncertainty.'

'I see.' The captain's tone had altered, and there was sympathy in his eyes as he glanced at Bella. 'I am afraid that Lionel Bromley was among the hostages taken by the Khan of Shapoora.'

'We know that,' Resaldar nodded. 'At one of the *dāk* stages near the border our guides heard about the hostages, and about the rumours that the Khan of Shapoora was using them in order to gain the throne of Afghanistan. We decided to carry on to the British headquarters to see what news we could gather about Lionel Bromley, but soon after we crossed the border we were captured by bandits. When they, in turn, were attacked by the Koku Khel, my sister and I tried to escape by dressing in *chadori*, but the Koku Khel spotted us and forced us to herd the sheep they had stolen.'

'I'll rustle up a pair of breeches and a shirt for you,' the officer said. Bella gained the impression that he was concentrating on practical matters, because there was something else which he was reluctant to tell them. He turned to her. 'As for you, Miss Haverington, we have nothing suitable, I'm afraid—'

'I'm wearing my own clothing underneath the *chador*,' she answered impatiently. 'Captain, what happened about the Army's scheme to put the Khan of Shapoora on the throne in return for the hostages?' Belatedly, she remembered what her principal preoccupation was supposed to be, and amended—'What I really mean is—what happened to the hostages?'

The officer cleared his throat, and did not meet her eyes. 'I'm afraid that all the hostages have been murdered.'

She stared blankly at him, and then a low moan escaped her. Her agonised thoughts were fixed on Simon, so that she had scant concern to spare for the others.

How *could* they have been killed? They had seemed so secure, hidden away in what should surely have been the complete safety of their caves. Unless the Pathan nomads had, after all, betrayed them—

Then she heard the captain go on, 'Before the Khan of Shapoora could set out with the hostages, to hand them over to the Army, the village was attacked and overrun by tribesmen led by the Khan's great-uncle. It has been established that every occupant of the village was killed, and that must include the hostages.'

Overwhelming relief coursed through Bella, and she was glad that the *chador* hid her expression from the captain. The death of the hostages was no more than an assumption on the part of the Army. The latter had no notion that the hostages had escaped immediately after the attack on the village began.

She half-turned towards Resaldar, and knew by the bleakness of his eyes that he was reflecting on the savage end of his former subjects, the tribesmen of Shapoora. Then she remembered that she was supposed to have been engaged to Lionel. Injecting a note of pathetic hopefulness into her voice, she said,

'You can't be absolutely certain that the hostages are all dead, captain. Can you?'

'I'm afraid we're as certain as it's possible to be. You see, in accordance with tribal custom, the dead bodies of the vanquished were placed on a pyre and burnt. By the time our scouts went into what remained of Shapoora there was nothing left by which to identify anyone. But we do know that the Khan of Shapoora had somehow escaped the holocaust, for the invaders were particularly looking for him, and since all the Afghan chiefs currently have bands of tribesmen scouring the area for him, it must mean that he is still alive. I shouldn't like to be in his shoes if the tribesmen find him before we do.'

Bella shuddered, and lowered her head in an attitude which suggested dumb grief for the loss of her fiancé. She listened as Resaldar questioned the captain.

'You, yourselves, are engaged in the search for the Khan of Shapoora?'

'Yes. We were making enquiries in the Pass when the murderous Koku Khel attacked and killed some of our men. We had scouts who knew how to reach their mountain retreat, so we postponed the search for the Khan and came to await the return of the Koku Khel.'

'The Army,' Resaldar mused, 'wishes to punish the Khan for the death of the hostages. But from what you have told us, Captain, he had intended honouring his bargain—'

'If he had not kidnapped them in the first place,' the officer pointed out grimly, 'they would be alive now!' He addressed himself to Bella. 'Have no fear, Miss Haverington! Your fiancé's death will be avenged. Major Cavagnari will personally see to that, for the daughter of his old friend, General Prewitt, was among them.'

She merely nodded mutely, her head still bowed. She had complete faith in Resaldar's instincts by now, so that it would not even have occurred to her to blurt out that the Army was mistaken, that the hostages were not dead, and that Resaldar was trying to reach Gandamak so that he might be proclaimed Emir-elect. Instead, she listened in silence as he said,

'The death of the hostages is a dreadful thing, and I absolutely agree that the Khan of Shapoora must pay for his part in it. But all the same, I would have thought that he was still too useful to the Army as a potential Emir, being half-English and so likely to serve the interests of Britain.'

'Not at all.' The captain smiled sourly. 'The Army sadly miscalculated the feeling among the tribes. They will not countenance a Christian Emir.'

'The Khan may well be prepared to convert to Islam—'

'That would not do him the slightest good. However publicly he might convert, the tribes would always suspect that at heart he remained a Christian. They would never trust him.'

So much, Bella thought sadly, for Resaldar's noble and passionate desire to bring religious tolerance to his country.

The captain was clearly caught up, now, by the subject under discussion. 'If they had asked me—' he shrugged. 'But of course, the top brass always think they know everything. They thought the tribes could be forced to accept any Emir who had the backing of the British Army. The result is that the Khan of Shapoora has now become a terrible embarrassment to them. Not only have the tribes made it clear that they will not countenance him at any price, but Yakoob Khan, who had been the first choice as Emir-elect, has decided to accede to all of the Army's terms.'

'Yakoob Khan is to be the new Emir?' Resaldar's voice was rigidly controlled, and only Bella could guess at the emotions which he was blotting out.

The captain nodded. 'All the chiefs have been arriving at Gandamak for the *Durbar* at which he is to be proclaimed Emir. The Army wants, at all costs, to prevent it becoming known just how far they had gone in conspiring behind Yakoob Khan's back while he was still considering their proposals, and that's why we're all searching so desperately for the Khan of Shapoora. The Army wants to silence him, using the deaths of the hostages as an excuse.'

Bella could scarcely bear to contemplate the anguish and frustration which Resaldar must be enduring beneath his air of casual interest. Deliberately, she allowed her attention to stray.

The soldiers had begun to set fire to the Koku Khel village. Some distance away the women and children of the murderous tribe watched with grim and silent defiance as their homes were destroyed. Despite everything, compassion welled up inside her, and she interrupted the captain impulsively.

'Is it really necessary to burn the village?'

'Indeed it is, Miss Haverington,' the officer assured

her. 'If we left it intact, this particular fastness would swiftly be infested by other mountain robbers. Don't trouble yourself about the women; they will merely disperse and move in with other villagers of the same tribe.'

He turned back to Resaldar, and took up their original discussion. 'You were saying, Mr Haverington—?'

'Merely that, in spite of myself, I find local politics fascinating. Do all the various tribes back this man, Yakoob Khan?'

'By no means! They're a raggle-taggle mob, constantly at one another's throats, and Yakoob Khan will have his hands full with them. But at least most of them are united in one thing. The notion of a half-English grandson of Shere Ali, and a Christian to boot, having had the temerity to aim for the throne has outraged them. Even without knowing how far the Army had already gone in intending to back the Khan of Shapoora, the tribes fear that at some stage the British might try to foist him upon them. They want him dead.'

'Well, I daresay he'll deserve whatever he gets,' Resaldar said with apparent unconcern, and changed the subject. 'If I could possibly have those spare breeches and shirt . . . I must confess, I have come to loathe the *chador*.'

The captain shouted a command to one of his men, and spare clothing was soon found for Resaldar. The men discreetly turned their backs as Bella pulled the ugly, enveloping *chador* over her head and shook out the creases in her gown. Then something in Resaldar's attitude alerted her to the dilemma which had suddenly been borne in upon him.

As a man, *he* could scarcely plead for privacy in which to change into his borrowed Western clothes. He would be expected to pull on the breeches there and then,

under cover of the *chador*. Then, having rid himself of
the bell-shaped garment, he could quite decently slip the
shirt over his head without offending the sensibilities of
Bella, the only female present, who was supposed in any
event to be his sister.

But as the two of them were only too well aware, the
chador concealed his own clothes. It would be quite
impossible to explain away the fact that he was wearing
calf-length pantaloons and a richly embroidered tunic
underneath the *chador*. Such items of clothing could
only form part of the wardrobe of an Afghan of high
standing. Someone like a hunted, half-English
Khan . . .

Bella looked wildly about her for inspiration. The
Koku Khel village was now well ablaze, and some
distance away soldiers were putting up tents and generally preparing to bivouac for the night.

She became aware that the captain was staring
curiously at Resaldar, who had still made no attempt to
divest himself of the *chador* which he'd affected to
dislike so much. She did the only thing she could think
of. Covering her face with her hands, she began to sob
noisily. Resaldar was swift to recognise and seize upon
her ruse.

'My poor sister,' he murmured. 'The shock of Lionel's
death has only just fully sunk in. I wonder, Captain, if I
might take her to lie down in one of the tents?'

'By all means!' the officer said sympathetically. 'I shall
put my own tent at your disposal. My batman will take
you to it, and give you some laudanum from the medical
supplies for your sister.'

Apparently still sobbing uncontrollably, Bella was led
away to the larger of the tents by Resaldar and the
captain's batman. The single-poled tent was carpeted
with coarse striped canvas and contained a bed-roll and

several charpoys. The middle-aged batman fussed over Bella with almost motherly concern, and it took all her ingenuity to avoid swallowing the laudanum which he pressed upon her, and to get rid of it when his attention was diverted.

But the batman's continued presence made it impossible for Resaldar to rid himself of the damning clothing which he wore beneath the *chador*. In desperation, Bella sat up on the bed-roll, her face still hidden by her hands. 'If I could have water—in which to bathe—'

'Well now, miss,' the batman said regretfully. 'Water is mighty scarce and is being saved only for drinking—'

'I'll go and see what I can find,' Resaldar put in swiftly. 'Perhaps there is a well in the village, not yet reached by the flames.'

The batman did not notice that, as well as the leather bucket, Resaldar took with him the borrowed breeches and shirt as he left the tent. To Bella's utter consternation, her feigned tears suddenly turned into a flood of genuine weeping, and she flung herself face down on the captain's bed-roll.

She recognised dimly that her tears were a reaction against everything that had happened—being captured by the Koku Khel and then rescued by the Army; the news that Resaldar was being hunted both by the Afghan tribes and the British, and then the final nerve-racking manoeuvring to get rid of the damning clothes he wore underneath the *chador*.

'There now, miss,' the batman soothed. 'The laudanum will soon start working and you'll fall asleep. Nothing will look quite so bad in the morning.'

After a while she *did* sleep, worn out by strain and tension and emotion. She awakened with a start and sat up, blinking in the guttering light of an oil-lamp. Movement caught her eye; beyond the light of the lamp someone was seated on one of the charpoys. The batman, still keeping a motherly eye on her . . .

He rose and came towards her, and she uttered a sound of confusion and alarm. It was not the batman. It was a Resaldar she had never seen before, and one whom she did not instantly recognise.

The tight-fitting breeches and shirt showed a tall, lithe figure which his voluminous *shālvar* trousers and embroidered tunics had always formerly disguised. Someone had cut his hair for him in the western style, so that it moulded itself to his skull like a tawny helmet. The beard and moustache which he had perforce been growing since they fled from Shapoora had been shaved off, so that his strong, tanned features contrasted sharply with the intense blueness of his eyes.

No one who had not previously been acquainted with him would have doubted for one moment that he was John Haverington, the heir to Haverington Hall in England. No woman of any age could have failed to experience a fluttering of the heart at the sight of him, so tall and spare and honey-gold of skin and hair, and yet with some untamed quality, bequeathed to him by his Afghan blood, in those startling blue eyes.

Unaccustomed shyness assailed Bella. She uttered the first words which entered her head. 'You—got rid of your clothes, then.'

'Yes. I wrapped them in the *chador* and tossed the lot into the blazing village without anyone noticing.' He gestured towards a table in a dim corner of the tent. 'It was decided not to wake you for supper. But there is bread and goat cheese and cold green tea. You must be hungry.'

'Yes.' She rose from the bed-roll and went to the table, and began to eat ravenously. But mindful of the tears she had been shedding, and the dishevelled appearance she must be presenting, she saved some of the cold tea so that she could bathe her face and her eyes, and then ran her fingers through her curls.

'How silent the camp is,' she said after a while. 'It must be very late. Where are you expected to sleep, Resaldar?'

'The captain thought I would wish to keep vigil over my grief-stricken sister.' His voice sounded strangely toneless.

'I see.' She struggled to speak casually. 'You could scarcely have made any valid objection to that.' She looked up at him, and suddenly the shyness which she had felt at his altered appearance vanished. She said quietly, 'I am so very sorry that your hopes of ruling over Afghanistan have come to nothing.'

He nodded, his expression bleak. 'At best, Yakoob Khan will be a weak ruler who will fail to unite the tribes. At worst, he will follow in the footsteps of his father, Shere Ali, and rule by savagery and terror.'

Bella sighed, and then concentrated on the one bright spot in the present situation. 'Resaldar, you look so completely the English gentleman that no one will now connect you with the Khan of Shapoora. You could return to England as John Haverington and take up your rightful position as heir and master of Haverington Hall—'

'No,' he interrupted quietly. 'You have forgotten something, Arabella. I could slip out of Afghanistan as John Haverington only if you and I remained utterly and for ever silent about the others.'

'The others?'

'Your brother—Flynn—Fawzia—the hostages. I couldn't possibly let the Army know where they are hiding without having to disclose who I am. And then, because I am now an embarrassment to the British, and it is important that they should establish good relations with the Afghan chiefs, I would have to be publicly executed.'

Bella looked mutely at him, unable to respond.

'The alternative,' he went on, 'would be to leave the hostages to their fate, with a limited supply of food, with no weapons and no means of transport. It would mean condemning them to death.'

'Oh, dear Lord . . .' she breathed, closing her eyes.

'So,' Resaldar's voice came to her, 'after all our desperate scheming to keep the truth from the captain, I must now go and tell him that I am the Khan of Shapoora. I must surrender myself into his custody, and ask him to send men in the morning to escort the hostages to safety.'

He placed his hands on Bella's shoulders. 'Once I had faced what I would have to do, I delayed only so that I could tell you first. We—have to say goodbye now, Arabella.'

Keeping her at a distance, he leant forward and touched his lips to her cheek. With a blind movement she closed the gap separating them and pressed her body close to his, sliding her palms in an urgent, desperate caress along his spine, feeling the tautness of his thighs under her fingers.

Beads of sweat had formed on his brow. He tried to push her away. 'Arabella, let us put an end to this. I must go—'

'No! Please . . . Let us have tonight. It will make no difference to the hostages if you surrendered in the morning. *Please* . . .'

With a sound of mingled despair and desire he laid his hand upon her throat and bent his head, seeking her lips, and she told herself that she had gained one night to be set against all eternity. One night of memories which would have to last her for the rest of her life.

With their lips still locked together they sank down on to the bed-roll. But with an abrupt, almost violent movement Resaldar put her away from him and rose.

'No, Arabella. You must marry someone else when all this is over. Lionel Bromley, perhaps. He is a good man, and I know that he loves you. You need someone to love you. I cannot bind you so irrevocably to me that you will be unable to give even part of yourself to some other man. It would be unforgivable of me.'

Tears were coursing down her cheeks. 'Please don't leave me,' she whispered. 'Not yet . . .'

Resaldar hesitated. 'It's late, and there is no real point in creating a dramatic situation at this time of night. I'll surrender myself into the captain's custody in the morning. Go to sleep now. Arabella, and I shall make myself as comfortable as I can on the charpoy.'

She sat up and drew her knees up to her chin. 'No. If tonight is all that is left to us, and you won't—' she broke off, and then continued. 'At least let us talk. I don't want to waste one second—' her voice cracked.

He began to talk at random. They discussed everything under the sun except their personal feelings, or the fate which awaited Resaldar in the morning. Bella told him about Haverington Hall, and about her life there.

'I was the family drudge. Your grandfather said I was destined to be an old maid, so I would have to earn my keep. I more than earned it, believe me!'

'He must have been an extremely unpleasant man,' Resaldar commented. 'What about my grandmother?'

'She died when she was not yet forty. It was quite sudden; she had not been ill. It's my belief that she willed herself to die, simply to get away from Great-Uncle Howard. He seemed to take her death as a personal affront; his overriding emotion at her funeral appeared to be fury. I remember how shocked my mother was that he shed no tears.'

'I daresay my grandfather blamed all the weaknesses of his son on my grandmother's side of the family,' Resaldar guessed shrewdly, and then sighed. 'There's no doubt that my father *was* weak.

'Even when I was quite small, whenever I watched him jumping to obey the commands of the Infidels, I wanted to scream at him to resist, to defy them, to be a man. My *mother* defied them in small, subtle ways which they could never quite pin down.'

'Did your mother ever regret the sacrifices she had made for your father?'

'My mother was not a woman who would have wasted useless emotion on regretting anything.' Resaldar's eyes shone with pride. 'I wish you could have met Shazeen. Even under the most miserable conditions she never forgot that she was the daughter of Shere Ali, or that she belonged to the Dooranee tribe, the most powerful tribe in all Afghanistan.

'She made sure that I did not forget it either. "Never let them see you weep," she used to say to me. "Never give the Infidels the satisfaction of knowing that they have the power to hurt or debase you." So, whenever I was forced to perform some menial task for the Infidels I told myself—"I am doing this because I have to, but I am a Dooranee and of Royal blood, and one day my turn will come." I drew strength from the tales my mother tole me about the Dooranee tribe.

'They possess a large tract of country between Kandahar and Herat, and each chief lives in a grand walled residence surrounded by the tents of his servants and henchmen. Kandahar used to be the seat of government until the legendary Timur had it moved to Kabul.'

'I remember being taught by my governess that

Kandahar was built by Alexander the Great.' Bella listened to herself making prosaic conversation while deep inside her despair was mounting. Already a pearly light was sifting into the tent, heralding the approach of dawn. Soon a bugle would be sounding reveillé to awaken the camp. And by tacit agreement she and Resaldar were spending these last few precious moments in discussing generalities.

'My mother made Kandahar come alive for me,' Resaldar was saying. 'I could see in my mind's eye the *chaursoo*—a domed building dominating the city, from which the Emir's proclamations used to be read out, and where the dead bodies of criminals were exposed to public view. And she described to me the tombs of my forefathers, Achmed Shah and his twelve children . . .'

They were silent for a while. The silence only seemed to emphasise the inexorable passing of time, and Bella sought desperately for something with which to fill it.

'Tell me how you came to be betrothed to Fawzia,' she said at last. 'You mentioned once that she is a princess of the Hazara tribe.'

Resaldar nodded. 'The Hazaras are of Tartar blood, descendants of Genghis Khan. Their domain is the Hazarajat, deep in Central Afghanistan. I came upon their country as a youth, while the tribesmen of Shapoora were still roaming Afghanistan, and I was still a slave. The chief of the Hazaras, Ubaidullah, is Fawzia's father. He became my ally and friend, and promised to do everything in his power to help me on to the throne of Afghanistan.'

'In return for marrying his daughter . . .' Bella murmured. She thought of Fawzia and Simon and the others, who could have no notion that their imminent rescue would be achieved only at the cost of Resaldar's life.

A sudden thought struck her. 'Resaldar,' she said urgently, 'would it be quicker for a rescue party to reach the hostages from here, travelling through the mountains? Or would a contingent of armed soldiers from Gandamak reach them sooner?'

'It would be quicker and more direct to travel from Gandamak—'

'And how long would it take you and me, escorted by a party of cavalry, to reach Gandamak from here?'

'With fast horses, and by joining the route at the nearest point, no more than two days or so. Why?'

'Because,' Bella said eagerly, 'in that case there is nothing whatever to be gained by surrendering yourself to the captain this morning!'

Resaldar frowned at her. 'You're suggesting that we should go to Gandamak as Mr and Miss Haverington, and that I should surrender myself to Major Cavagnari himself? What on earth would be gained by that?'

'*Time*,' Bella said with intensity. '*Hope*. Please, Resaldar! Something might happen between here and Gandamak—'

'Nothing will happen,' Resaldar contradicted flatly. 'It would merely be putting off the evil day.'

But after some argument, he was persuaded to say nothing to the captain. Instead, soon after reveillé, Resaldar approached the officer with a request that he and Bella should be escorted at once by a party of cavalry to Gandamak.

'I should like,' Bella interposed, injecting a note of suppressed emotion into her voice, 'to collect my poor Lionel's personal effects and then leave Afghanistan as soon as possible.'

'An understandable sentiment, Miss Haverington,' the captain agreed sympathetically. 'Very well. An escort will be detailed to take you to Gandamak.'

The sure-footed Army ponies picked their way down the track soon afterwards, and they entered a gorge scattered with ancient rocks. Sometimes the track descended to the level of a winding river, and they were able to stop and water the horses. All around them the red cliffs reflected the fierce heat of the sun.

Apart from meeting several parties of nomads, and once engaging in a short and half-hearted skirmish with a band of hostile Afridis, nothing whatever happened during the journey. There was certainly nothing to fulfil Bella's hope that extra time would bring some solution to the agonising dilemma facing them.

Towards the end of the second day they reached Gandamak. As if to present them with a dreadful omen, their arrival at the British camp coincided with the public execution of four Pathans who had been found guilty of murdering one of the Army's camel-wallahs.

The culprits were tied hand and foot, and placed with their backs towards the firing party, a bamboo rod to which their wrists were bound keeping them close together in a straight line. The order rang out to present arms and a moment later the wretched prisoners went down like so many dominoes, each man having received four bullets in the back.

What made the whole scene even more gruesome was the fact that it was being witnessed, as if it were a spectacle laid on solely for their entertainment, by a large audience of Afghans in jewel-encrusted turbans and silken robes. Each dignitary was surrounded by what were clearly servants, some fanning their masters with elaborate constructions of vellum and bird feathers.

'The tribal chiefs,' Resaldar said tersely in Bella's ear. 'They are obviously awaiting the triumphant arrival of Yakoob Khan as Emir-elect.'

'Avert your face,' Bella pleaded fearfully, 'lest some of them should recognise you.'

'Would it matter?' Resaldar returned in a cynical voice.

'Yes, it *would*! If—if you are to be executed—' she swallowed. 'The British way would be quicker, more humane . . .' Her voice caught.

He put out a hand, and touched her arm briefly. 'Don't think about it. And have no fear that the Afghans will recognise me and claim a prior right to put me to death. My uncle, Wali Mahomed, was the only one of the chiefs who could have identified me in person. And he, if not killed at Shapoora, would have been sufficiently badly wounded not to have been able to attend the *Durbar*. As for the others—'

He stopped, and sucked in his breath sharply. Bella saw that his gaze was fixed upon one of the reclining chiefs, a man with flattish features and slanted eyes.

But before Resaldar could say any more, a soldier came to tell them that Major Cavagnari was ready to receive them.

'My dear Miss Haverington,' the Viceroy's Plenipotentiary addressed Bella as they were ushered into his tent. 'I have been told of your sad loss. Indeed, I can feel for you the more because the daughter of my good friend Clive Prewitt perished at the same time as your fiancé. The hostages—'

He broke off, frowning, his gaze searching her face. 'We have met before, surely?'

Bella was about to confess bleakly that she had first made his acquaintance dressed as a boy, when she felt Resaldar's fingers biting painfully into the flesh of her arm, clearly conveying a warning.

'That is quite impossible, Major,' she heard Resaldar say smoothly. 'This is my sister's first visit to Afghanistan and will assuredly be her last. We came to enquire whether we might take the personal possessions of Lionel Bromley back to England with us.'

Totally bemused, Bella listened as Major Cavagnari explained that Bromley's personal effects were at Jellalabad.

'But to save you a further exhausting journey,' he continued, 'I shall issue orders for them to be brought to Kabul.'

'Kabul?' Resaldar frowned.

'Why, yes. As soon as Yakoob Khan arrives, and formally tenders his acceptance of the British terms, the war will be over. I shall then accompany him with an escort on a triumphal procession to Kabul, and you will join us as my guests. You will, I think, find that the capital offers some degree of comfort in an otherwise bleak and inhospitable country.

'Now,' he added with a polite but dismissive smile, 'I am sure that both of you must be very tired. I shall have tents placed at your disposal.'

After they had left Major Cavagnari's presence, and were following a soldier towards a row of tents, Bella asked in utter confusion, 'Why—why did you not tell him who you are, Resaldar?'

There was a note of elation in his voice. 'Because you were right, my dearest Arabella. Something *has* turned up. Among the tribal Khans was one whom I had no expectation whatsoever of finding here. I can still scarcely believe that he has left his remote domain to attend the *Durbar*. But he has, and in him I can see my deliverance!'

'Whatever do you mean, Resaldar?'

'Ubaidullah is here. Fawzia's father. He will help me. Already I have thought of a way of rescuing the hostages without putting my own life in peril.'

CHAPTER
NINE

RESALDAR WOULD not go into details about his plans. 'There is no time,' he told Bella. 'I must try to gain an audience with Ubaidullah before the evening devotions, and I must do so in a discreet and very unobtrusive way.'

There was no question of Bella being able to accompany Resaldar. Not only would she have hampered him, but since Ubaidullah could speak no English there would have been no point in her being present during Resaldar's interview with him. So Bella resigned herself to waiting inside her tent with such patience as she could muster, while Resaldar set out to make secret contact with Fawzia's father.

'Perhaps,' Bella had recommended anxiously, 'it would be best if you were to let him believe that I truly am engaged to Lionel Bromley. If he suspected that you and I—'

Resaldar had given her a ghost of a smile, understanding her perfectly. 'This is Afghanistan, remember. Provided I did not dishonour Fawzia by casting her off, her father will not care how many other romantic involvements I might enter into. Now, stop fretting and await my return.'

But it was difficult *not* to fret while she waited. Since Ubaidullah cared so little for his daughter that he would have her locked away, or even perhaps have her murdered, if Resaldar cast her off, might he not also turn quite as ruthlessly against Resaldar himself now that the latter stood no chance of becoming the Emir of Kabul?

Bella's breath escaped in a release of tension as the tent flap moved aside, and Resaldar entered, a triumphant light in his eyes.

'Ubaidullah has pledged his support! He is setting out with his men in the morning, and will hurry to the caves near Shapoora where the hostages are hiding. He is using the imminent arrival of Yakoob Khan as his excuse. Ubaidullah is one of the Khans who voted against Yakoob Khan as the Emir-elect. When I left him he had already sent a messenger to Major Cavagnari, giving notice that he means to absent himself from the forthcoming ceremony. It will arouse no suspicions; Ubaidullah will not be the only Khan who will not wish to stay and see Yakoob Khan recognised—'

They were interrupted at that moment by one of Major Cavagnari's personal staff. The Viceroy's Plenipotentiary was inviting them to dine with him and a few other senior officers, and with typical military efficiency had obtained formal clothes for the occasion for both of them.

Bella had no doubt whatsoever that the beautiful gown which she lifted from its wrapping of tissue-paper had come from one of the numerous trunks which had left England with Nicolette Prewitt, and she suppressed a stab of guilt as she thought of the bereft feelings which must have accompanied General Prewitt's offer of his daughter's gown for her use.

Nicolette would soon be restored to him, Bella told herself. As yet she did not know how Ubaidullah was to accomplish this without implicating or endangering Resaldar, and it was impossible to find out at the moment, for Major Cavagnari's valet was offering to help Resaldar with his evening toilette in his own tent. It was an offer which Resaldar accepted with a gratitude which perhaps only Bella recognised, and it struck her again how totally unfamiliar he was with western customs of dress or behaviour.

Left to herself, Bella bathed and washed her hair in the hip-bath of hot water which a batman had carried in for her. Major Cavagnari—or more probably General Prewitt—had thoughtfully sent over a shaving mirror so that she could, at least, inspect part of her appearance. Someone had also donated a pair of his hair-brushes, and with their help she coaxed her unruly curls into restraint, so that they softly framed her face as they dried. She would not have been human if she had failed to experience a thrill of pleasure as she contemplated stepping into Nicolette's gown.

Of white silk, it was trimmed with lace embroidered in pearl beads. The low-cut bodice was arranged in narrow puffs divided by similarly embroidered panels and the train was lavishly trimmed with marabou feathers. Because it belonged to Nicolette, and they were of the same size, Bella knew that it would fit her to perfection.

But there were seemingly overwhelming obstacles to her wearing the dress. In the first place, no suitable undergarments had been provided, and Bella's own much-laundered and decidedly down-at-heel chemisette would not have done. It would have been visible in all its shabbiness above the neckline of the dress.

Biting her lip with disappointment, Bella contemplated sending word to Major Cavagnari that she could not, after all, accept his invitation to dinner. She could plead Lionel's recent death as her excuse. Since Major Cavagnari had obviously forgotten the fact that she was supposed to be in mourning, he would guiltily acknowledge that she had a valid reason for refusing the invitation.

And yet, she *wanted* to go, and she yearned to wear Nicolette's beautiful gown. She thought of approaching General Prewitt and asking him to lend her some suitable undergarments belonging to Nicolette. But instinct told her that the General would be thrown into acute embarrassment by the request. Also, it might draw the officer's attention to the fact that she was not precisely behaving like a grief-stricken girl mourning her fiancé's recent death.

Rashly, Bella decided to wear the gown without a camisole. Her waist was trim and lean, her bosom firm enough for none but the most keen-eyed female to notice the absence of an undergarment.

Her mind made up, she stepped into the gown, and encountered another apparently insurmountable problem. The gown fastened with tiny pearl buttons down the back, and they were impossible for Bella to reach. It was a gown which absolutely demanded the help of a ladys' maid, another fact which had occurred to neither Major Cavagnari nor General Prewitt.

Bella pulled on the gown's matching white slippers, and then sat down on the truckle bed to consider the matter. She knew that the wives and daughters of the officers had all been left behind at headquarters at Jellalabad. But she had noticed the presence of some half-dozen determined camp followers, ladies of dubious virtue. Sooner or later the batman would return to tidy the tent; when he did, she would ask him to send one of these women to help her.

In the meantime, Bella draped a blanket about herself, and occupied the time while she waited by detaching some of the marabou feathers from the train of the gown and fashioning them into a decoration for her hair, which would otherwise have presented too stark and unadorned a contrast with the richness of the gown. Although unorthodox, the effect of the bunched feathers among her curls was curiously attractive and seemed to accentuate the auburn tints in her hair.

A shadow fell across her and she looked up, dropping the mirror on the bed, Resaldar stood framed in the opening of the tent. He wore a starched white shirt and a black tail-coat with rounded revers, cut short in the front, together with matching black slim-fitting trousers. The resourceful valet who had helped him to dress had even procured for him a buttonhole of some local violet-blue flower which echoed and intensified the colour of his eyes. But it was something quite apart from the elegance of the clothes which lent such splendour to Resaldar's appearance.

It was the regal way in which he held himself; his innate sense of being Shere Ali's grandson, of being part of a Royal dynasty. His clothes might proclaim him to be John Haverington of Haverington Hall; his bearing was that of the Afghan Khan of Shapoora, a member of the powerful Dooranee tribe, a legitimate Pretender to the throne of Afghanistan. The two halves of his identity, fused like that, produced an effect so devastating, so electrifying, that Bella could only stare mutely at him.

Completely unaware of the effect he was having upon her, he frowned slightly and entered the tent. The two lanterns which the batman had lit threw a golden halo of light about his tawny hair.

'It would be foolish to offend Major Cavagnari by being late,' he said. 'Why are you not ready, Arabella?'

Briefly, she explained that she could not button the gown. 'Please ask someone to send one of the camp followers to help me,' she added.

Resaldar shook his impatiently. 'Stand up. I'll button your gown.'

'It would be most improper. If the batman should return and see you—'

He looked down at her, his eyes dark and raw with what looked like anger but which she recognised as frustration and desire and bitter self-denial.

'You are meant to be my sister,' he reminded her in a thick voice. 'Nothing could seem more proper if anyone should enter. So stand up, and let us have done with it.'

'You don't understand—'

Impatiently, he stopped, placing his hands under her arms and pulling her to her feet. As he did so the blanket fell to the ground, and the unbuttoned bodice of her gown slipped from her shoulders, so that the lamp-light played on her naked flesh.

A muscle jerked beside his mouth. 'Turn round,' he said tersely.

She obeyed, her body trembling. Manlike and un-handy, he chose to begin with the lower buttons and she could feel his warm, unsteady fingers moving from one small pearl button to the next. His breathing was un-even, stirring the curls in the nape of her neck. When he reached her waist, she felt his hands grow still.

He made a strangled sound. His hands moved from the hollow of her waist to cup her naked breasts. She drew a long, ragged breath and tilted her head so that it rested on his shoulder and his mouth covered hers, probing and insistent, sending flames of passionate long-ing and need coursing through her.

They were still locked in mutal anguish of pain and loss and forbidden desire when the sound of approaching footsteps brought them back to sanity. They were supposed to be brother and sister. They dared not be caught in anything approaching a compromising situation.

With an outward show of composure, but with shaking hands, Resaldar was completing the task of buttoning her gown when the batman entered to tidy the tent. Bella had grabbed the mirror and was pretending to pat her curls into place so that her expression would not betray her.

Afterwards, her arm tucked lightly into Resaldar's, they left the tent. Neither of them spoke as they set out to join Major Cavagnari and his guests for dinner.

The large, double-poled tent was almost the size of a marquee. Among the guests were General Sir Sam Browne and Generals Maude and Prewitt. Neither of the latter showed a glimmer of recognition as Bella and Resaldar were introduced to them; they obviously did not connect her in any way with the youth named Stanley Fullerton whom they had previously met.

Major Cavagnari explained genially to his two non-military guests, 'The dinner tonight is by way of being a celebration. We received a message by sun telegraphy today that Yakoob Khan will arrive in the morning to tender his submission to the British Army. He will then be formally acknowledged as the new Emir, and the war will be over.'

Bella could only guess at what Resaldar must be feeling, for his face was totally impassive. Even so, she hastened to make conversation, afraid that he might be betrayed into giving himself away.

'I have never been quite certain, sir, of the reasons for the war in the first place,' she addressed Major Cavagnari.

'You are not the only one, my dear Miss Havering-ton,' he answered with some cynicism. 'Most of the Afghan tribes, themselves, were under the impression that the British had invaded simply to rid them of Shere Ali's oppression, and would thereafter obligingly depart. It has been almost impossible to make them understand our aims for a "scientific frontier".'

'And what is that?'

'It is simply a means of securing that the British Government would have the power to enter Kabul whenever necessary,' the Viceroy's Plenipotentiary explained. 'With Yakoob Khan's agreement to have a British Resident installed in Kabul, and with our scientific frontier firmly established, Russia will never in future years be able to impose its will upon Afghanistan or invade the country.'

'Yakoob Khan will prove to be a weak ruler,' General Maude forecast pessimistically. 'He will meet with considerable opposition from many of the tribal chiefs. There are revolutionary elements in Afghanistan, and I doubt if he'll last long.'

'Nonsense! The Army will stay on after the Peace Treaty has been ratified. Our forces will be concentrated both at Gandamak and at Lundi Khotal in the Khyber Pass to see that Yakoob Khan is not toppled from the throne.'

'All the same,' General Maude persisted, 'I think the Army blundered in backing Yakoob Khan. We should have forced the tribes to accept that young upstart, the Khan of Shapoora.'

General Prewitt made a violent sound. *'Damn his black, murdering soul!'*

The other officer immediately apologised. 'I forgot myself for a moment, my dear Clive. But rest assured, the scoundrel can't possibly escape punishment for the tragic death of your daughter. Both the Army and the Afghans are energetically looking for him, and sooner or later he'll be found and brought to book.'

'Yakoob Khan,' Major Cavagnari put in reflectively, 'has asked most particularly that his nephew, the Khan

of Shapoora, should be handed over to him as his
prisoner, no matter who runs him to earth. I understand
these Afghan fellows have a charming habit of burning
their enemies alive. Something to do with damning the
poor devil's soul eternally in the after-life, and rendering
him unfit to become a martyr.'

'Good!' General Prewitt muttered vengefully. 'Let
Yakoob Khan have him! We British are far too squeam-
ish to see that the blackguard suffers as he deserves to!'

Bella held herself rigidly. She glanced at Resaldar; he
was staring impassively into his glass of Madeira.

Major Cavagnari decided to give the conversation a
less morbid turn. He congratulated Bella with heavy
gallantry on her appearance, and apologised for the lack
of female company or frivolous amusements about the
camp. Then, snapping his fingers, he exclaimed,

'It has just occurred to me, Miss Haverington, that it
might amuse you—' he stopped, and went on apologet-
ically—'How crass of me. I have been forgetting entirely
that you are in mourning for your fiancé. You will not
wish for amusement, frivolous or otherwise.'

Bella looked down at her hands, and murmured,
'Lionel would not have wanted me to wallow in grief, sir,
or lock myself away, and it was for that reason that I
accepted your kind invitation to dinner.'

'Good! Capital!' Major Cavagnari said with relief. 'In
that case, would you and your brother care to witness the
ceremonial arrival of Yakoob Khan in the morning? It
would, I must warn you, entail making a very early
start.'

Bella glanced helplessly at Resaldar. Could he
possibly endure with fortitude, and without betraying
himself, the triumphant arrival of the uncle who was to
be proclaimed Emir in his stead? The uncle who wished
to have him burnt alive so that not only would he cease to

be a possible future rival for the throne, but also to prevent him from becoming a martyr to the other tribes?

With that intuitive understanding which existed between them, Resaldar answered for her. 'It would certainly be interesting to witness the arrival of the new Emir. I'm sure neither my sister nor I would mind making an early start in order to be present at such a historic occasion.'

The rest of the dinner party continued upon pleasant, conventional lines. Bella noticed that Resaldar was swift to learn, by watching the others, how to cope with the bewildering array of cutlery and glasses surrounding his plate, and no one would have guessed that this was the first formal western dinner he had ever attended.

The evening came to an early end, as everyone present would be riding out in the morning, to meet Yakoob Khan. Resaldar accompanied Bella to her tent and, with rigid self-control this time, unfastened the buttons of her gown. As soon as the last loop had been detached from its corresponding pearl, he bade her a curt good night and left.

Only when she had stretched out upon the truckle bed did Bella remember that she still had no notion of how Fawzia's father, Ubaidullah, would accomplish the matter of delivering the hostages safely to the Army without betraying Resaldar's identity. She shivered as she thought of the fate which awaited him if he should be unmasked.

With the hostages safely restored, the British Army could not—even if it should want to—do anything to save Resaldar. For the sake of good relations with Yakoob Khan the Army would have to turn him over to the new Emir.

The thought kept her awake for so long that she had barely slipped into an uneasy doze before a batman called discreetly to her from the flap of the tent that it was time to rise if she wished to join the procession which planned to meet Yakoob Khan on his way to Gandamak.

The early morning air was bitterly cold. Bella found the camp to be a seething hive of activity. Not only were the various regiments preparing for the procession and the subsequent reception of Yakoob Khan, but Ubaidullah's henchmen were mustering their camels and packing them up, preparatory to leaving the camp. As Resaldar had forecast, some of the other Afghan chiefs, too, were pointedly absenting themselves from the ceremonious arrival of Yakoob Khan, and were getting ready to leave by routes which would avoid meeting their unwelcome new Emir along the way.

Seated upon the white mare which had been lent to her by the Army, Bella was joined by Resaldar, similarly mounted.

'We're to ride with Major Cavagnari and his escort of native Sowar Guides and 10th Hussars,' he informed her without expression. 'In a dip in the road between the Red Khotal hills and the bridge at Surkhab, the meeting with Yakoob Khan is scheduled to take place. Major Cavagnari will hand Yakoob Khan a *khareeta*—an official letter from the British Viceroy addressed formally to *Emir Mahomed Yakoob Khan, Wali of Kabul*, thus recognising him as the ruler of all Afghanistan.'

Bella gave him a look of sad regret, and he returned it with a small, bitter smile. 'I mourn for Afghanistan, and not for myself,' he said. 'It will not be long before convulsions again shake my poor country.' Then he shrugged. 'But by that time I shall, hopefully, have established myself as John Haverington of Haverington Hall in Sussex.'

Bella searched his face. 'Do you think you will be able

to adjust? You know nothing of life in England, and you have always scorned the thought of making it your home.'

He laughed bleakly. 'I no longer have a choice, have I? I shall be forced to adjust. If I remained here as Resaldar Khan I would be put to death by the new Emir. My very life depends on my becoming John Haverington and exiling myself to England.'

She knew that he was right, but she could not help wondering how he would settle down to life as a country squire in England. Then her thoughts turned to other matters.

'Resaldar,' Bella asked in an undertone, as they cantered towards where Major Cavagnari's party were mustering, 'how will Ubaidullah explain his return to Gandamak with the hostages, without involving you?'

'He won't be returning to Gandamak,' Resaldar told her. 'We are all shortly to leave for Kabul, remember? Presumably as part of an official party escorting Yakoob Khan to the capital, to see him installed in the Royal palace.'

Bella nodded, frowning. 'So Ubaidullah will be taking the hostages to Kabul—'

'No. His men will rescue the hostages, and then take them to the Buddhist caves near Kabul—those same caves to which my mother Shazeen and my father escaped, and in one of which I was born. As soon as they have reached the caves safely Ubaidullah will return to his own domain in Central Afghanistan, and Flynn will send me a pre-arranged message.'

'Go on,' Bella urged.

'I shall then tell Major Cavagnari that I am the Khan of Shapoora and that the hostages are alive and unharmed. As the price of their freedom, I shall demand a promise of immunity and safe conduct to Britain as John Haverington.'

Bella chewed uneasily on her lower lip. 'How do you know that Major Cavagnari can be trusted to give you safe passage once the hostages have been returned?'

Resaldar favoured her with a slightly taunting smile. 'My dear Arabella, what a question to be posing to a barbaric Afghan in connection with an English officer and gentleman! I have always understood that men of Major Cavagnari's ilk pride themselves on never breaking their given word!'

'No,' Bella conceded. The Viceroy's Plenipotentiary would be furious at having been deceived and outwitted, but he would stand by his promise.

She thought of her young brother, and said anxiously, 'You're sure that Ubaidullah and his men will be able to bring the hostages safely to the caves near Kabul? I had always envisaged a military escort for them—'

'The Hazara tribesmen,' Resaldar reminded her drily, 'are descendants of Genghis Khan. The most fearsome of the marauders infesting the Khyber Pass would tangle with a British military escort far more readily than they would with Ubaidullah and his henchmen.'

Bella nodded, satisfied. She sat in silence for a moment, her hands engaged in aimlessly twisting together the reins of her horse. Without looking up, she said, 'What—what of Fawzia? When her father first promised her to you in marriage, it was in the expectation that you would one day be the Emir of Kabul . . .'

'Fawzia,' Resaldar returned in a voice which was now completely devoid of expression, 'will travel to England with me. She will take instruction in the Christian faith, and when she had been baptised and confirmed we shall be married.'

Bella looked up then, and saw the pain in his eyes. 'It

cannot be any other way,' he said quietly. 'Ubaidullah is more than resigned to her leaving the country and abandoning Islam. Indeed, it has now become a matter of great pride to him that she is to be the mistress of an English mansion.'

Resaldar smiled thinly. 'He has it fixed in his mind that his daughter will daily be hobnobbing with Her Majesty, Queen Victoria. The thought gives him considerable satisfaction.

Bella nodded mutely. There was no way out for them. Even if Ubaidullah were not helping to save Resaldar's life, Fawzia could not be abandoned to her fate.

There was no further opportunity for discussing the matter, because Major Cavagnari and the others were ready to leave the camp, and she and Resaldar had to take their places in the procession.

The sun rose, sending mist curling like smoke into the air. All along the right side of the route which the procession was to take, the cavalry were drawn up and waiting to attention.

When they reached the spot where the first meeting between Major Cavagnari and Yakoob Khan was to take place, Bella saw that a Fakir had constructed a kind of triumphal arch by slinging a rope across the road, with a copy of the Koran tied in a cloth suspended in the middle. In this way the new Emir of Afghanistan, Wali of Kabul, would have to pass beneath it and so be blessed.

And then Yakoob Khan and his escort came into view. Very dignified and correct they looked as they rode towards the meeting place. Yakoob Khan, Bella saw, was a man of some presence, with aquiline features and dark hair and beard. But there was something weak or perhaps merely careworn in his features, and his skin had an unhealthy, sallow look to it. She had learnt that he had spent long years of imprisonment under the orders of his late father, Shere Ali, and that the experience had taken its toll of his health. If she had not known of the fate which he had in mind for Resaldar, she might have felt a stirring of compassion for him now as he advanced to meet the Viceroy's Plenipotentiary.

'*Khub hasti?*' Major Cavagnari enunciated carefully.

'Are you well?' Resaldar translated in a whisper for Bella's benefit.

'*Salamat bashi,*' Yakoob Khan responded formally. '*Mandeh nabashi.*'

'May you be healthy. May you never be tired.'

Leaning out of the saddle, Major Cavagnari shook hands with the new Emir and his accompanying ministers. Then the whole party moved towards Gandamak where, on the height leading to the Valley of Surkhab, General Sir Sam Browne and his staff were waiting. Beyond them, standing to attention, troops lined the route on either side for at least three miles, stretching as far as the watercourse known as the Gandamak Nullah.

After the formal ritual of shaking hands with General Sir Sam Browne, Yakoob Khan and his suite, followed by the British officers and their staff, slowly rode down the lines. The band struck up the British National Anthem, and Yakoob Khan and his following sat rigidly in their saddles until the last strains of *God Save the Queen* had re-echoed off the surrounding mountains.

As the procession approached the river, the forty-pounders thundered a twenty-one-gun salute. Near the Royal tent which had been prepared for Yakoob Khan, the Royal Horse Artillery and the mountain guns were drawn up with the rest of the 10th Hussars, while a battalion of the 17th was stiffly at attention opposite the entrance to the Royal tent.

All this display of military pomp and dignity could have given Yakoob Khan no hint of the misgivings with which the British Army was acknowledging him as Emir. His own guard of soldiers, highlanders of very tall stature, and dressed in dark green tunics over long skirts of homespun tartan, immediately stationed themselves possessively and defensively around the Royal tent. Yakoob Khan dismounted and disappeared with his attendants into Major Cavagnari's tent to partake of refreshments with the top military brass. The ceremonial fanfare was over.

A sense of anti-climax gripped the camp after that. While Yakoob Khan retired to his own tent, the Army began to make all the practical preparations which attended the ending of a war. The big guns were dismantled and many of the tents were struck, for the large majority of the troops were to leave immediately on the homeward march, and would be staying at standing camps along the route. Some of the regiments would be remaining at Gandamak as a peace-keeping force, but it was hoped that, with the British supplying Yakoob Khan with money and arms, he would swiftly subdue the unruly tribes so that the Army could withdraw completely before the year was out.

A few days after Yakoob Khan's arrival, the Treaty of Peace was ratified. Salutes of honour were fired at Gandamak, and Bella learnt that guns were simultaneously resounding over Kabul, the capital. Preparations were being made to escort Yakoob Khan to that city.

Bella and Resaldar were among the party which accompanied Major Cavagnari on the journey to Kabul. Although the war was officially over, bands of unruly marauders were still looting villages in the name of Islam and in defiance of the choice of Yakoob Khan as Emir.

The Sowar Guides accompanying Major Cavagnari, together with Yakoob Khan's highlanders, dealt with these isolated hostilities whenever they met them, so that as far as Bella and Resaldar were concerned the journey was almost uneventful.

At last they reached the capital of Afghanistan. Situated upon the river of the same name and dominated by towering mountain peaks, the city of Kabul was entered by a narrow street, intricately criss-crossed by other streets, all equally badly paved.

Bella's bemused attention was caught by the numerous shops, some little better than sheds, which lined the streets. Here vendors were exhibiting fruit of many different kinds and in lavish abundance. There were dealers in carpets, lace, furs and saddlery; merchants were offering for sale guns and swords, silks and sugarcane, all with a splendid disregard for the fact that the procession which they were importuning to buy their wares consisted of the ceremonial escort of their new Emir.

Major Cavagnari positioned his horse so that he was riding abreast of Bella. 'We shall soon have left this noise and squalor behind us, Miss Haverington.'

She did not like to admit that she had been totally fascinated by what he termed noise and squalor, and returned a non-committal reply.

'We are bound for the *Bala Hissar*, or Palace of Kings, a citadel in which are the Royal residence and gardens. It is almost a town in its own right inhabited by some five thousand people, most of them Government officers or members of the ruling Dooranee tribe and their servants and henchmen. Outside the city are the tombs of the Emperor Babar and of the legendary Timur Shah. You must try to visit them before you leave Afghanistan.'

'I very much hope,' Bella ventured, 'that I shall have

an opportunity to explore the bazaar and some of the shops while I am in Kabul. Chaperoned by my brother, of course,' she added hastily.

Major Cavagnari pursed his lips. 'It might be considered a strange and eccentric desire by the women of Yakoob Khan's household. Especially,' he emphasised with a sideways glance at her, 'for a young woman who is here on the melancholy mission of collecting her late fiancé's belongings.'

'Of course,' Bella agreed, chastened. She would really have to try and remember that she was supposed to be in mourning for Lionel Bromley.

The procession was now approaching the wall which surrounded the *Bala Hissar*. The height of this wall was regulated according to the rise and fall of the surrounding mountains, and contained numerous bastions. The procession passed through an open gate which led into the town of kings, and Major Cavagnari pointed out the *Musjid Shahee*, or Royal mosque. Bella acknowledged the information politely, and then manoeuvred her mount in such a way that she would ride close beside Resaldar in the procession.

Keeping her voice low, she asked, 'Do you think Simon and the others will have reached the Buddhist caves in safety by now?'

He nodded. 'I gave Ubaidullah a note to deliver to Flynn. Ubaidullah was to leave one of his men behind at the cave, to act as Flynn's messenger. It was arranged that the man would come to the *Bala Hissar* as soon as the others are safely installed in the cave, and ask for John Haverington. He will announce that he has a piece of property belonging to Lionel Bromley, and that he understands the Haveringtons will pay a reward for it. He will then hand me Bromley's neckerchief, with some story of having found it in the ruins of Shapoora, and I shall pay him a few rupees. The messenger will then depart.'

'And that will be the signal for you to tell Major Cavagnari that you are the Khan of Shapoora?'

'Yes. Once I have Major Cavagnari's promise of immunity and safe passage out of Afghanistan, I shall lead him to the cave.'

Bella chewed at her lip. 'How long do you suppose we shall have to wait for the messenger to arrive?'

'I daresay he will be awaiting us at the *Bala Hissar* even now. But, to avoid suspicion, he will probably remain in hiding for a few days before he announces his arrival and asks for John Haverington.'

The procession was beginning to split into groups. Yakoob Khan and his entourage made their way towards the magnificent gardens which surrounded the Royal palace, while Major Cavagnari's party headed towards an imposing building which was, very shortly, to be occupied by the new British Resident. At present it was to be put at the disposal of Major Cavagnari, his staff and his friends.

Servants, obviously forewarned, emerged from inside the residence and, with many salaams, began to escort Major Cavagnari's party inside. General Prewitt, who had been the first to reach the door, stood aside so that Bella could precede him. She had no more than a swift impression of carved pilasters and exquisite wooden carvings when what seemed like a tornado hurled itself across the entrance hall and fell upon General Prewitt's neck.

'Papa! Oh, dearest Papa!'

The room spun around Bella. When she had regained some measure of control over her senses, she saw that Simon and Lionel Bromley were moving towards her, smiling broadly. Flynn held back, and Fawzia in her black *chador* and veil was almost invisible in the shadows of the room.

'Bella!' Simon cried exuberantly, and flung his arms about her. Then he stared at Resaldar. 'Good lord, I scarcely recognised you, Cousin!'

Major Cavagnari, his voice slightly bemused, took control of the situation. 'You, I take it,' he addressed Simon, 'are one of the hostages—by some miracle, alive.' He turned to Resaldar. 'But why did you not tell me that your cousin was also among the hostages, Mr Haverington?'

Before Resaldar could form a reply, Flynn strode forward. His expression was guileless, and he sketched a respectful salaam in Resaldar's direction. Then he turned to Major Cavagnari.

'*Mr Haverington?*' he echoed. 'Sure, and didn't you know who ye're after addressin', sir? Why, 'tis none other than himself—His Highness, Resaldar, Khan of Shapoora!'

Something, Bella thought numbly, had gone dreadfully wrong. Flynn had misunderstood Resaldar's instructions. Her brother and Lionel were beginning to detect undercurrents in the atmosphere, and were frowning uneasily. Nicolette detached herself from her father's embrace at last, and ran to Flynn, placing her hand on his arm.

And as Bella looked up into the Irishman's face, and saw the glint of calculation in his eyes, she recognised the truth.

Flynn had not misunderstood. He no longer had anything to gain by helping Resaldar, and therefore he had betrayed him.

He had, quite deliberately and in the full knowledge of what he was doing, delivered Resaldar into the hands of his enemies.

CHAPTER
TEN

THE SILENCE which followed Flynn's calculated and almost casual betrayal was broken by an excited jabbering among the servants. They had caught the title '*Resaldar, Khan of Shapoora*' and they understood sufficient English to realise that this blue-eyed, western-looking man, despite his tawny-gold hair and skin, was the legendary, hated enemy of almost all the Afghan tribes.

Major Cavagnari recovered himself. 'Are you,' he demanded of Resaldar, 'John Haverington, or are you the Khan of Shapoora as the Irishman claims?'

'I am both,' Resaldar returned resignedly.

Major Cavagnari shook his head, and said in a bewildered voice, 'But your sister—'

Resaldar looked at Bella. 'She is not my sister. She is my—' he broke off. For one long moment their glances were locked in wordless communication. *You are my love*, his eyes were telling her. *We shall not see one another again. I am saying goodbye to you, my love.*

'She is my cousin,' he continued aloud, his voice flat.

'Your cousin? *Your cousin!*' Realisation dawned slowly in the eyes of the Viceroy's Plenipotentiary.

He snapped his fingers, and whirled about to face Bella. 'The so-called youth who delivered this upstart's demands to me at Gandamak in the first place! I *knew* I had seen you before!' His face darkened. 'You sought to trick the British Army, madam! By God, I'll—'

He did not complete whatever angry threat had been hovering on his tongue. Instead, he called sharply to the Sowar Guides who had stationed themselves on guard at the entrance to the residence, and commanded them to seize Resaldar.

'Take him to the Palace,' Major Cavagnari said curtly, 'and deliver him to the Emir with my compliments!'

Bella watched in numb despair as Resaldar was clapped into irons, and taken away. Perhaps, the tormented thought ran through her brain, perhaps Major Cavagnari would have been more prepared to be merciful if he had not been so angry at Bella's own deception. He might have been persuaded to allow Resaldar to be smuggled out of Afghanistan as John Haverington . . .

But no, common sense insisted. Apart from the fact that the house servants had heard Flynn proclaiming Resaldar to be the Khan of Shapoora, one only had to look at the vengeful anger on General Prewitt's face to know that *he* would never have been party to an attempt at helping Resaldar escape.

She heard Flynn clear his throat. Gently, he removed Nicolette's hand from his arm and approached General Prewitt.

'Sir, I should like to introduce myself. I am Seamus Flynn, at your service. 'Tis with the greatest personal satisfaction I restore your daughter to you, sir, because she has come to mean every bit as much to me as she does to yerself!'

'Oh, Papa, he was simply *splendid*!' Nicolette interrupted adoringly. 'It was he who led us all to safety after we had been captured by a band of ruffianly tribesmen! They drove us into some caves, and then set an armed bandit to guard us while they, no doubt went to see what other wretched prisoners they could find to hold to ransom. But my darling, courageous Seamus over-powered the guard, and disarmed him, and quickly led us from the caves!'

With a strange, unreal detachment, Bella noted the different expressions chasing one another across General Prewitt's face. Reluctant gratitude towards Flynn; the knowledge that he was indebted to a man he despised, and the extremely unwelcome realisation that his beloved, pampered daughter had called him her 'darling Seamus'.

With a self-deprecatory gesture, Flynn said, 'Sure, and I simply did what had to be done.'

At that moment the numbness which had enveloped Bella cracked. She flew across the room like a fury, her fists flailing at Flynn's chest, kicking his shins with all her might, fighting off the hands which sought to restrain her.

'You black-hearted—treacherous—Irish *devil*!' she gasped. 'You contemptible rat! You were given Resaldar's note—you knew why Ubaidullah and his men were leading you to the Buddhist caves! It was no armed guard you overpowered—it was the man Ubaidullah had left to act as your messenger, and well you knew it!'

Strong arms grasped Bella from behind, and pulled her away from Flynn. 'Please try to calm yourself, my dear,' Lionel Bromley said gently.

'Indeed, Miss Stanley,' she heard Flynn murmur in unctuous, humouring tones, 'I don't know of what ye're after accusin' me at all.'

'*Miss Stanley!*' Major Cavagnari echoed, his voice hard. 'So even your name was a lie, madam! And it is clear, from your rambling accusation, that you were thoroughly in cahoots with your Afghan cousin throughout! What is this about Ubaidullah? I take it you were referring to the chief of the Hazara tribe?'

'He was Resaldar's ally,' she answered tonelessly.
'We knew that Resaldar had only one chance of escaping
from Afghanistan—by using the hostages to bargain for
his freedom. So Ubaidullah and his men set out to rescue
them from the caves near Shapoora where they were
stranded, and brought them to the Buddhist caves near
Kabul. There they were to have remained in complete
safety until Resaldar led the Army to them in exchange
for his freedom.'

'We knew nothing of this,' Simon said in a dazed
voice. 'It's true that tribesmen came, and drove us from
the caves near Shapoora. We thought they were capturing us. Flynn said nothing about having been handed a
note! *The damned blackguard*—'

'Fawzia!' Bella exclaimed, and turned to the girl who
was still hovering in the shadows. '*You* must have known
that they were your father's men! *You* must have
realised that they had come to rescue you and not to
capture you!'

'I knew they were my father's men,' Fawzia confirmed, her voice stoically resigned. 'But they did not
confide in me. It would not have been fitting, for I am a
mere female. As for my father—' she shrugged. 'He
embraced me before he left for his own domain, and said
I was about to set off on a long, long journey, and that we
should never meet again. I thought he was sending me
into exile, because I had been cast off by Resaldar Khan.
What else *could* I have thought?'

'We were all in such utter ignorance,' Lionel Bromley
put in. 'Hiding in the caves near Shapoora, we had no
notion of what was going on in the rest of the country.
And when the tribesmen arrived and made it clear that
they were taking command of us, we assumed we were
their captives. None of us saw Flynn being handed
Resaldar's note, or knew of its existence.'

'Indeed, and there *was* no such note,' Flynn said smoothly.

'Of course there wasn't!' Nicolette confirmed. 'As far as that ruffian, the Khan of Shapoora, was concerned, we could have rotted there in the caves after he left with Miss Stanley! My brave Seamus was trying to devise a plan for leading us to safety when the tribesmen swooped on us, and drove us practically at pistol-point through that wretched country, and imprisoned us in yet another cave!' She shuddered. 'Heaven alone knows what our ultimate fate would have been if dearest Seamus had not overpowered the guard and then led us to Kabul and the *Bala Hissar*.'

Bella turned a blazing, contemptuous gaze on Flynn. 'If you had not received a note from Resaldar, then how could you possibly have known that you should lead the others to the *Bala Hissar*?'

He shrugged. Clearly, he had been anticipating the question. 'Sure, and it did not take long after we'd left the Buddhist cave before I learnt that Yakoob Khan had been proclaimed Emir. I understand the language, after all, and I discovered that the Viceroy's Plenipotentiary was to escort him to the *Bala Hissar*. I guessed that General Prewitt would be with the escorting party, and that is why I brought the hostages here.'

Major Cavagnari took control of the situation, and put an end to the exchange. He favoured Bella with a look of intense dislike. 'Unfortunately, it does not fall within the scope of the Army's powers to punish you for your part in this dastardly business. But you will be leaving Kabul immediately, this very day. You and your brother will be taken to join the first of the troops departing for England, and you will travel under their protection.'

'Please,' she begged, her lips numb. 'Please—let me

stay until I—until Resaldar—'

'Has been put to death?' he supplied with blunt distaste. 'If I were an uncivilised man, Miss Stanley, I would do precisely that as a punishment for you! But you know how Yakoob Khan will deal with your cousin. He will have him burnt alive. Whatever else you are, whatever you have done, you *are* an Englishwoman, and to save you from having to witness that grisly spectacle I am sending you home immediately!'

General Prewitt cleared his throat. 'I should like Nicolette to accompany you on the journey, Miss Stanley. You would each serve as chaperon to the other—'

'No, Papa!' Nicolette protested passionately, and cast an ardent glance at Flynn. 'Oh no! I do not wish to leave just yet! There are matters which Seamus and I have to discuss with you, and besides, I want to see something of Kabul after the dreadful ordeal I have been through! You must let me stay!'

General Prewitt chewed his lower lip, a frown creasing his brow. His reactions were totally transparent. He wished to remove his beloved daughter from Flynn's orbit without delay. At the same time, he had never been able to deny her anything. And something in her expression must have warned him that he would stir up an ungovernable storm if he tried to force his will upon her in this instance.

'Well,' he gave in weakly, after a moment. 'We shall see.' He glanced at Major Cavagnari. 'Since Miss Stanley is, in any event, not eager to leave Kabul immediately, I should like to ask that she remains for the time being as a companion and chaperon to Nicolette. Since she is the only other British female at the *Bala Hissar*—'

Major Cavagnari interrupted him with an irritable

shrug. 'As you wish, my dear Clive. Now, I am exceedingly weary of the whole sorry affair, and I have official business to attend to. If you will all excuse me—'

He strode away, accompanied by salaaming servants. General Prewitt made to follow, but Nicolette said urgently, 'Papa—Seamus and I wish to speak to you in private.'

Wearing a hunted look, General Prewitt nodded and addressed one of the hovering servants. 'I believe a suite of rooms have been put at my disposal—'

'Sir!' Salaaming, the man turned to lead the way and General Prewitt followed with Nicolette and Flynn.

'Oh, the low-down cur!' Bella ground out as her eyes followed the Irishman from the room. 'If only I had warned Resaldar . . . I sensed, from the first moment I met him, that Flynn would always turn every opportunity to his own advantage!'

'His motive, in this case, is glaringly obvious,' Lionel said soberly. 'Resaldar's note must have made it clear to him that Yakoob Khan had been proclaimed Emir. Flynn no longer had anything to gain by helping Resaldar. And at the same time Nicolette, the only child of a very wealthy father, had become violently infatuated with him, and he saw the chance of presenting himself in a good light to General Prewitt. Oh yes, I understand his reasoning. I only wish I hadn't been such a fool as not to suspect something of the truth before now!'

One of the servants who spoke English coughed discreetly and suggested that everyone should follow him to partake of the refreshments which had been prepared for Yakoob Khan's honoured guests. Mechanically, Bella followed the others into a chamber with stuccoed walls and moulded ceilings and rich furnishings in the Oriental style.

Female servants, wearing fragile silk veils which masked their faces, ushered Bella and Fawzia into an adjoining room and brought green tea and small cakes which Bella ignored. She stared at Fawzia, whose eyes—the only feature left visible by her veil—were as impassive as ever.

'Don't you care,' Bella asked harshly, 'that Resaldar is at this very moment imprisoned in some dungeon beneath the Palace, knowing that he is to be tried and then burnt alive?'

A sigh escaped Fawzia. 'Naturally I care. But it is the will of Allah. We must accept these matters.'

No! a voice screamed inside Bella's head. *Never!*

For a long while she sat with her face buried in her hands. Then she looked up. 'What will you do now, Fawzia? Now that Resaldar—'

'I cannot return to the Hazarajat, my father's domain,' the girl answered with quiet resignation. 'And because I have been under Resaldar Khan's protection since I reached womanhood, no one else would marry me now. There will be no place for me anywhere. I shall join the outcasts and the beggars and place my trust in Allah.'

'No!' At least, Bella thought feverishly, here was a focus for her attentions, something with which to occupy her mind, even temporarily, for if she continued to do nothing but contemplate Resaldar's fate she would surely go mad.

'No,' she said again, less vehemently. 'You will go to England with Simon and me. There will be a home for you at Haverington Hall. I suppose—' her voice cracked. 'The Hall will pass to Simon after Resaldar—well, in any event, you will live there as of right. That was what your father meant when he said you were to go on a long journey, and never see him again.'

Fawzia contemplated the proposition in silence for a moment. 'There is a mosque near this Haverington Hall, and Mullahs to interpret the Koran?'

'No. I'm afraid that you would have to convert to Christianity.'

Fawzia sighed again. 'It is the wish of Resaldar Khan and of my father that I should go to this Haverington Hall?'

'Oh yes! I know that your father wished it, and I'm quite certain that Resaldar would be desolate if he thought that his—that his death would leave you an outcast . . .'

'You love Resaldar Khan,' Fawzia interrupted. It was a simple statement of fact. 'Poor Bella, it is hard for you.' She was silent for a long while. Then she said reflectively, 'You are convinced that I must abandon Islam, and embrace Christianity instead, even though I am not to be married after all?'

'Well—you need not embrace Christianity if you don't want to, but there would be no possibility of your practising Islamic law. There are people in England, Fawzia, who do not follow any particular religion—'

'No, I cannot be an Infidel!' Fawzia fingered her veil with regret. 'I shall convert. If only I did not find your creed so—so informal, so lacking in mystique . . . It will be strange to have no taboos, to make no sacrifices.'

She started as the cry of a *muezzin* reached them. 'I must go and make my devotions,' she said and rose to leave.

Oh God, Bella thought with anguish, *if only I could be like Fawzia. If only I could find comfort in ritual, and accept everything as the will of the Deity . . .*

She was still sitting there, staring unseeingly at her untouched refreshments, when she was joined by

Nicolette. 'Well,' the girl said with satisfaction. 'Papa has not precisely given in—but then I never expected him to do so immediately. However, he has promised to give the matter very careful consideration.'

'What matter?' Bella responded mechanically.

'Why, my engagement to Seamus, of course!'

Bella made a sound deep in her throat. 'How you can even contemplate marriage to such a rat—'

'I will not have you disparage him!' Nicolette cried fiercely. '*You* of all people! Don't imagine that I do not know what must have passed between you and that—that half-breed cousin of yours!'

Bella stood up and walked out of the room, possessed by a blind rage which included Nicolette, Flynn, and fate itself.

In the adjoining room, she found that her young brother was toying with his own food just as she had been doing. He looked up at her, and she could tell that he was fighting back tears.

'Bella,' he said hoarsely, 'how long do you suppose it will be before they—before Resaldar—'

'I don't know.' Her own mouth worked, and she hurried to escape.

Outside, she found the gardens embellished with fountains and planted with shady trees. But the restful atmosphere which they were meant to induce had no effect on her. She was staring unseeingly into the waters of one of the fountains when she heard a footfall behind her, and turned her head.

It was Lionel, his eyes filled with compassion and with love. 'Oh, my poor dear Bella,' he said simply.

With a muffled sob, she turned to him. He held her while she wept. A long while afterwards, when she was capable of speech, she looked up at him with tear-drenched eyes.

'Lionel—is there any hope—*any whatsoever?*'

'I'm afraid not,' he answered honestly, for there was no way of softening the truth. 'Yakoob Khan will have Resaldar burnt at the stake, just outside the walls of the *Bala Hissar*. Oh, there will be a *Durbar* beforehand, a kind of trial, if you like. But the result is a foregone conclusion. Resaldar's death will have to take place, in public and with maximum ostentation, not only to remove any possible threat he might present to Yakoob Khan, but also as a warning to the other members of the Royal family not to cast envious eyes upon the throne and try to further their aims with the help of the British Army.'

'I—see.'

'Oh, Bella!' He held her to him. 'I've told you before, I'm an ordinary kind of fellow. I don't cut a dash. I'm not capable of great, heroic gestures. And I know that I would always only be a poor second best. But if you could—when all this is over—'

She managed a twisted smile. 'That was what Resaldar once said. That I—that I should marry you. But you are too good to have to accept second best, my dear Lionel, and I—' Her face worked, and she had to swallow hard before going on. 'I could not—even pretend to be a wife to you or to anyone else—after loving Resaldar . . .'

He sighed. 'I do understand, my dear.' His bleak gaze scanned the Royal palace in the distance, and suddenly he burst out with unaccustomed vehemence, 'Damn and blast Nicolette Prewitt with her infatuation for the Irishman! If she were not insisting on staying at Kabul, to try and talk her father into agreeing to their engagement, you could have been spared the ordeal of facing the inevitable—'

'I *wanted* to stay,' she reminded him.

'You don't know what it will be like,' he said grimly. 'You will have to watch the pyre being built outside the walls . . .' He shook his head. 'But there, General Prewitt will not countenance an alliance between his daughter and Flynn, and he'll pack her off home in a day or two.'

But in that Lionel was proved wrong. Whatever private arguments and tantrums were being enacted between Nicolette and her father, the girl remained in Kabul, and no preparations were made for her leaving. And because she wished to see as much of Kabul as she could, under Flynn's escort and protection, Bella was forced to accompany them as a chaperon.

As she trailed behind Nicolette and Flynn, Bella remembered how eagerly she herself had once wished to explore the strange, narrow streets with their numerous shops and stalls. Now it was no more than a wearisome chore as she followed the other two to one of the kebab shops.

The proprietor was seated in the centre, superintending the cooking and also serving his customers. A servant chopped meat in one corner and placed it on skewers, while a ragged small boy fanned the charcoal fire. There was no lack of customers, who bought the kebabs and consumed them seated in the open street. The poorer Afghans appeared to live mostly out of doors, sleeping huddled against some chance wall or other, buying their food from a kebab shop if they were in funds or else joining the many beggars who appealed insistently for alms in the name of the Prophet.

'Those, Miss Stanley,' Flynn said condescendingly, including Bella in his guided commentary to Nicolette, 'are the *kuttars*.'

She turned her head listlessly and followed his pointing finger. A string of blind beggars were filing along in a slow crocodile, holding on to one another by the shoulders.

'The man leading the *kuttars* has one eye,' Flynn observed. 'Himself it is who collects the alms. More often than not the spalpeen makes off with all the spoils, and leaves the blind ones to their fate.'

Bella gave him a direct look. 'If *you* were a one-eyed man in Kabul, Mr Flynn,' she said stonily, 'you would find a ready-made vocation.'

He shrugged off the insult. 'Let us pay a visit to the *fulloodeh* stall, he suggested to Nicolette, and Bella was forced to follow.

The stall was neatly and tastefully fitted out. A pillar of snow stood in one corner and a fountain played behind it, while large earthenware pots of flowers and loaves of sugar were arranged on either side.

'*Fulloodeh*,' Bella heard Flynn's voice, 'is sometimes called *Rahūt-i-jān*, the solace of life. It is a refreshing drink made of a kind of jelly strained from wheat, mixed with snow-water and sherbet or sugar.'

Pain, sharp and terrible, washed over Bella as she remembered the night in the *rabat* when Resaldar had pretended that *fulloodeh* was potently intoxicating. He had tormented her and forced her to reveal her true sex; then he had made her wear Nicolette's gown and teach him the waltz. And he had kissed her for the first time . . .

She turned away from the *fulloodeh* stall. 'I—feel faint. I'm sorry, but I can't play gooseberry any longer today.'

As they returned to the *Bala Hissar* in a hired conveyance Bella noticed with black despair that work had started on a pyre just outside the walls of the Palace of Kings. The pyre on which Resaldar was to be burnt alive . . .

She found Fawzia awaiting her return. 'Bella, an Army chaplain called today to speak to General Prewitt on some matter, and I had a long audience with him. He explained many things to me.'

'Yes?' Bella returned automatically.

Fawzia sighed. 'I can accept that Allah and Christ are but two names given to the same Being. But I cannot feel *right*—I cannot feel properly devout . . . Bella, could I not live at Haverington Hall as a Muslim, even though there is no mosque and no Mullah? Could I not retain the *chador* and veil, and practise the teachings of the Koran, and make my devotions privately? Who would be hurt by it if I did?'

Bella forced herself to give her full attention to the girl. '*You* would be hurt by it, Fawzia. You see, the people on the estate and in the nearby Haverington village—well, to them you would seem utterly alien and strange. They have never seen anyone wearing *chador* and veil before. Many of them are ignorant and superstitious—'

'Superstitious?'

'I'll try to explain. Not long ago they blamed every single misfortune which befell any of them on an old woman who used to live alone on the outskirts of the village. Her only crime was that she was a lonely stranger; I believe she had been someone's nanny, and had been pensioned off in this remote cottage. Well, merely because she had not been born there, because she kept to herself, and because she had a black cat as a pet, the local people decided that she was a witch and they persecuted her. They threw stones at her, or set their dogs on her, and once they tried to burn down her cottage. In the end she drowned herself in a brook.'

'But how dreadful!'

'Yes. Ignorance makes people cruel. So just consider

how the local inhabitants would regard *you* in your black *chador*, and with your face permanently hidden by a veil!'

Fawzia sighed. 'I suppose you must be right. I do not understand about life in England. I shall try to come to terms with what the chaplain has told me.'

In the days that followed, the pyre outside the *Bala Hissar* walls grew noticeably and obscenely higher. Bella could no longer sleep at night, and when she did fall into a doze she was tormented by nightmares.

Nicolette had taken to using Bella as a confidante, nightly invading her bedroom to prattle away about her affairs. Bella made appropriate noises but continued to think her own agonising thoughts.

One morning, in utter despair, she went in search of Lionel Bromley. 'A thought occurred to me during the night. Lionel, do you suppose that Yakoob Khan would grant you an audience?'

He stroked his chin. 'Yes, he probably would. He is very sensitive at the moment about what the British newspapers might print about him.'

'If you were to put it to him that Resaldar's execution would make a very bad impression on the British public—'

'No, Bella,' Lionel said definitely. 'That would not sway him. He would point out that in Britain enemies of the state are shot or hanged. Only the manner of the execution is different; the end result is the same.'

She twisted her hands together. 'Very well, then, could you ask him to grant *me* an audience? If I could plead with him, if I could point out that Resaldar is the son of his own sister Shazeen—'

'I doubt if he will agree to see you, my dear,' Lionel said gently. 'Do not forget that in this country women are regarded as lowly, inferior creatures. For an Emir to grant an audience to a female would be almost unheard of.'

She dropped her face in her hands, and said in a muffled voice, 'Then—then please just ask him—if I could see Resaldar for the last time . . .'

He touched her cheek gently. 'I'll do my very best.'

She waited, tense as a coiled spring, while Lionel set off for the Palace. He was gone for so long that a perverse hope began to grow in her heart. Lionel must be arguing with the Emir, making him see what an indescribable obscenity it would be to put Resaldar to death—

She saw his figure approaching from the direction of the Palace, and sped to meet him. Her footsteps slowed as she caught sight of his face.

'The Emir will not allow me to see Resaldar,' she said tonelessly.

'No.' Lionel folded her hands in his. 'And—there is something else I have to tell you—'

He looked away from her. 'The sentence is to be carried out the day after tomorrow. Resaldar has less than forty-eight hours to live.'

CHAPTER
ELEVEN

BELLA STARED mutely at Lionel, and he cursed under his breath. 'The devil take Nicolette Prewitt! All this added torment you are being put through—and for nothing! Never in a million years will her father consent to her marrying such as Flynn—'

'Oh, but you are wrong,' Bella broke in quite automatically, speaking only because in that way she could temporarily succeed in blotting out her own thoughts. 'Her father has consented.'

'*What?*'

'An official announcement is being prepared to be sent to newspapers in London. Flynn's reputation is being cleaned up and glossed over. He is being made respectable, you see; an acceptable husband for someone moving in Nicolette's circles. She threatened to run away and live with him in sin otherwise, and her father has had to bow to her demands.'

Lionel whistled. 'How on earth could *Flynn* be made to seem respectable?'

'He is to be given an official rôle in the Army, and a distant relative of his is to be used to lend him social status. The announcement of the engagement will read that Seamus Patrick Flynn, independent adviser to Her Majesty's Army in Afghanistan and cousin of Sir Michael Flynn of county Down, is to marry Miss Nicolette Prewitt.'

'I see,' Lionel said slowly. 'Yes, I see . . .'

Bella gave him a wavering smile. 'People like Nicolette always get what they want in the end.'

'So it would seem. I suspect she will live to regret having *this* particular wish granted.'

But Bella had no thoughts to spare for Nicolette's possible future disenchantment. In forty-eight hours Resaldar would be dead, put to death in the most horrifying manner.

The following day, Resaldar's last day on earth, Bella locked her door and refused to see anyone. Simon came and begged her several times to accept a tray of food in her room at least; Fawzia called gently to her through the keyhole that what was to happen was the will of Allah and had to be accepted as such. Nicolette knocked more strenuously on her door, and complained,

'You are being utterly selfish! Seamus wishes to take me to visit the tomb of Timur Shah, and Papa won't allow it unless I am chaperoned—even though we are now unofficially engaged! I wish you would think of someone other than yourself sometimes!'

Only Lionel seemed to understand Bella's need for private grieving, and left her alone.

At times she prayed; at others she wept in hopeless despair or pounded her fists against the wall in mindless rage against fate. And endlessly the thought pounded through her brain—how much had she, herself, contributed towards what was to take place in the morning?

Would matters have ended differently if she had not insisted on setting out for Afghanistan to find her lost cousin? Would Resaldar have abandoned his ambition for the throne of Kabul if he had not been provided with heaven-sent hostages, British cousins who were wandering through the Khyber Pass, drawing attention to themselves by making enquiries about his village, and accompanied by the daughter of a high-ranking Army officer?

It grew dark, but Bella would not admit the servants who called to light the lamps. She stretched out, fully-clothed, upon the bed and stared unblinkingly into the darkness. A clock on the bureau relentlessly ticked away the seconds, the minutes, the hours. She lay, listening for the hourly chimes, her grief-stunned mind calculating precisely the time which remained left to Resaldar.

Midnight had just struck when she heard footsteps in the passage outside, and someone knocked on her door. It was a peremptory, commanding sound.

'Miss Stanley! Open this door!'

Dazed, she recognised the voice of General Prewitt himself. Surely *he* would not concern himself with the fact that she had not eaten all day? Particularly not at this time of night . . .

Sheer surprise compelled her to go to the door and unlock it. He held a branch of candles in one hand and carried what appeared to be a bundle of clothing over his free arm. He was looking at her with intense dislike.

'Here,' he said brusquely, thrusting the bundle of clothes at her. 'Put these on and come outside.'

'What—? Why?' She looked stupidly at the bundle of clothes.

'It is the uniform of a boy soldier,' General Prewitt said, and added with angry irony—'*You* should not feel too out of place in it! Come along—hurry!'

'But—why? What is happening?'

'Your wretched cousin has been allowed to escape, but he is by no means out of danger. If you wish to save his life, change into this uniform and join him and your brother outside, and leave Kabul. Quickly!'

Bella's thoughts were scattering, fragmenting, refusing to take in more than one consideration at a time. 'Fawzia—' she began. 'We can't leave her behind—'

General Prewitt swore under his breath. 'Very well! She will be provided with a similar uniform! Now, change your clothes quickly, and then go and assist her!'

In a state of complete mental disorientation, Bella closed the door and dressed in the uniform of a British boy soldier. There was just sufficient moonlight slanting through the gaps of the shutters to allow her to see what she was doing.

Still understanding nothing, she sped to Fawzia's bedroom afterwards. The girl was making clumsy attempts to button her tunic. 'Bella,' she appealed, 'why is it necessary for me to wear these clothes? I feel so confused, so—indecent. The clothes show my—my *shape*—'

'I don't know what is going on. I can't take it in either. Stand still, Fawzia, and let me hide your hair underneath the cap.'

'Resaldar Khan has been freed,' Fawzia said in a bemused voice. 'That is all I have understood. He is not to die at the stake in the morning.'

'No.' For the first time the true extent of the miracle flooded Bella's being, leaving her breathless. Then she forced herself into brisk action.

'Come. General Prewitt said that speed was essential.'

Silently, they hurried through the deserted corridors. Whatever was going on, the house servants were not a party to it. When they reached the main door to the residence they found Lionel guarding it.

'Resaldar and Simon are waiting for you outside with spare horses,' he said rapidly. 'A contingent of Sowar Guides will ride with you, and take you to join one of the cavalry regiments leaving Afghanistan for the journey home to England. Until you are safely over the border you must appear to be four soldiers of the British Army.'

'Lionel—what has happened? How has this—this

miracle—come about? General Prewitt said that
Resaldar was *allowed* to escape—'

'There is no time to explain.' He embraced her swiftly,
and kissed her lips in sad farewell. 'You must hurry to
leave Kabul. In the morning, at the eleventh hour, it will
be "discovered" that Resaldar has escaped and a hue-
and-cry will be raised. You must be safely hidden among
the home-going troops by that time.'

He pulled a note from his pocket and tucked it inside
the pocket of Bella's tunic. 'Later, when there is time to
spare, my note will explain everything. Go now, and
Godspeed.'

The next hours passed in a blur of utter unreality.
Resaldar and Simon, mounted on horses and dressed as
British soldiers, were waiting with an escort of Sowar
Guides. There was no time for Bella to exchange so
much as a word with Resaldar; she and Fawzia were
speedily helped on to horses, and then they rode as fast
as they could from the *Bala Hissar*.

Except for the sleeping, homeless populace of Kabul,
the streets were deserted, and the horsemen were able to
make good time, assisted by a full moon. They rode
without rest or respite until some time after noon, when
they caught up with a cavalry regiment on its way to the
border. And even then there was no time to do more
than snatch a hasty meal, change horses and continue on
with the regiment, whose commanding officer had been
handed a letter from Major Cavagnari by one of the
Sowar Guides.

At last, towards dusk, the regiment reached one of the
standing camps, and bivouacked for the night. Bella
stumbled wearily from the saddle. She placed a consol-
ing, reassuring hand on Fawzia's shoulder, realising how
completely disorientated the girl must be feeling in her
disguise as a British boy soldier.

Together, they followed Resaldar and Simon to the tent which had been allocated to them.

Before there was any opportunity for private speech between them, the commanding officer visited their tent. His tone was neutral as he said,

'I am aware that two of the boy soldiers are, in fact, ladies. In future I shall try to ensure that a tent be put aside for your exclusive use, but for tonight I am afraid you will all have to share this one. Until we are across the border, it will be as well for you to appear nothing other than ordinary members of the regiment. Good night.'

He was gone before they could question him about the dramatic turn of events.

Even Fawzia was too tired, too numbed and confused by the turmoil of the past hours to protest at the prospect of sharing sleeping quarters with two males. In virtual silence, they sat down and ate their rations.

Only afterwards was Bella able to gaze at Resaldar, unfamiliar in his British uniform, and allow pure joy to course through her. He looked thinner after his imprisonment and there were dark shadows etched about his eyes. He met her gaze for a long moment of silent communication.

'Does anyone,' Simon demanded suddenly, 'have any idea whatsoever what happened, and why?'

Resaldar shook his head. 'I only know that I was brought from the dungeon beneath the Palace last night, issued with a British soldier's uniform, and then handed over to Sowar Guides.'

For the first time, Bella remembered Lionel's note, and retrieved it from her pocket. By the light of an oil lamp she began to read it aloud.

My dear Bella—by the time you peruse this you will, I hope, be safely out of Kabul with your brother and with Resaldar.

When you told me that General Prewitt had at last consented to his daughter marrying Flynn, and that our Irish friend was to be given a spurious respectability, I suddenly saw a way in which I might be able to gain for you your heart's desire.

I knew that, in spite of what Major Cavagnari might say to the contrary, if the Army really wished to save Resaldar they could do so. Every man has his price, and Yakoob Khan is no exception. Offer him a few more sophisticated weapons and a substantial increase in the financial aid originally promised to him by the Army, and he would be willing to allow Resaldar to 'escape'.

So I demanded to see Major Cavagnari and General Prewitt and, not to put too fine a point on it, I blackmailed them. If they did not procure Resaldar's release, I said, I would write a piece for my paper, exposing all of Flynn's unsavoury activities in Afghanistan. The matter of running guns to the tribes, of exploiting British soldiers, of being heavily involved in the capture of the hostages in the first place—all would be described in graphic detail, and the piece would be published at the same time as Nicolette's engagement to Flynn is announced.

Well, General Prewitt knew that not even my threats would induce his headstrong daughter to give up Flynn. And Major Cavagnari is his friend, his wife one of Nicolette's godmothers. Neither of them could stand by and allow the resultant scandal and ridicule. They were forced to give in to my demands. Yakoob Khan has received a massive bribe and, in the morning when the guards go to Resaldar's cell to drag him to the stake, it will be found that he had made a most amazing escape.

'I always knew that Bromley was a good and decent man,' Resaldar interrupted, shaking his head. 'I did not guess that he could be so brilliantly resourceful as well. I owe him more than I could ever repay.'

'It just shows,' Simon put in, 'there is truth in the saying that the pen can be mightier than the sword. Is there more to the letter, Bella?'

'Yes.' She began to read the concluding sentences of Lionel's letter aloud before she had realised their personal nature, and by then it would somehow have seemed to detract from what he had done for them all if she had stopped.

'I would have been more than content to be second best, but you wanted your heart's desire or nothing. Be happy, my dear, and when you have married Resaldar spare an occasional thought for your devoted and loving Lionel.'

Bella's voice cracked on the last words. What was it that Lionel had once said to her? *'I am not capable of great, heroic gestures.'* He had been utterly wrong . . .

Something had been pinned to the note, and as she turned it over she discovered that Lionel had added a postscript. *'You will all need a wardrobe of some kind before sailing, home, and so I attach a draft on my bank in Bombay. Pay me back if and when you are able to.'*

Tears stung Bella's eyes, blurring the words. Then she heard Fawzia's puzzled voice. 'I do not understand. Is it your wish to marry Bella, my Lord Khan?'

'No.' Resaldar's voice was strained. 'Lionel Bromley was under a misapprehension. I have no intention of marrying anyone but you, Fawzia.'

'Oh.' There was disappointment in her voice. 'I had hoped, Resaldar Khan, that you might marry us both, so that Bella and I could be as sisters.'

It was Simon who answered for him in scandalised tones. 'In England that would be immoral, Fawzia, as well as illegal!'

'And you must stop calling me Resaldar Khan,' Resaldar put in. 'In England I shall be known only as John Haverington.'

Fawzia sighed. 'I do not understand English ways at all.'

Abruptly, Resaldar closed the discussion. 'We are all tired. Let us wrap ourselves in our blankets, and get some sleep.'

The days and weeks which followed consisted of riding with the cavalry regiment through the Khyber Pass. Conditions were often gruelling, always uncomfortable and sometimes dangerous.

Whatever may have been decided at the Durbar at Gandamak, it was clear that to the majority of the tribes the war was continuing. One night the camp was attacked by a large body of Ghilzais. It became obvious that the enemy's plan was to draw off the troops in front while the camp would be rushed at the rear. Swift action on the part of the British command foiled the attack, but Bella and Fawzia shivered in their tent as they listened to the sound of gunfire.

As well as enemy attacks, they had to contend with the elements. When it rained water streamed through the sodden canvas of the tents and sent the single candle spluttering continually and occasionally going out, and everyone became soaked to the skin.

Even when they were approaching the end of the Pass, several of the camp followers who straggled behind were set upon and murdered. A charge of cavalry galloped to the foot of the hill into which the attackers had run, discharging their Martini-Henry carbines but the tribesmen melted effectively away into their natural habitat.

Resaldar's expression grew increasingly grim with each show of hostility, and Bella could guess what he was thinking. Yakoob Khan was too weak to unite the tribes and would not remain on the throne for long.

Apart from the fighting, their journey followed a grim routine, and Bella became so used to bivouacking at standing camps, falling into her bed-roll at night in a state of utter weariness and being roused by the unwelcome sound of the bugle at dawn that she almost forgot that she was *not* a boy soldier returning home after active service.

But at long last they had left the Pass, and were making for the railhead. In Bombay they only had time to spend Lionel's bank draft on basic necessities for each one of them before they had to board the steamer which was waiting to set sail for England.

The Army were paying their passages, and had even arranged that Bella and Fawzia should each have private berths. Simon and Resaldar shared quarters with the home-going troops.

Since there were no more than a handful of females travelling on the ship, Bella had expected to spend most of her days in Fawzia's company.

But instead, the other girl had struck up an acquaintance with a nursing sister who was returning from her duties at a field hospital in Jellalabad. Perhaps it was the sister's apparel which caused Fawzia to identify with her, for the nurse belonged to a Catholic order, and wore a black habit which was not too far removed from the *chadori* which Fawzia had only recently discarded so reluctantly, and the nun's wimple left scarcely more of her face visible that Fawzia's veil had been used to.

In any event, they appeared to have endless grounds for discussion, so that Bella saw very little of Fawzia.

Because she had nothing in common with the few other women on board, who were mainly disillusioned camp followers, and because Simon and Resaldar were confined to the troops' quarters, the voyage was a lonely one for Bella, and she could not help contrasting it with the excitement of the outward voyage on board the P & O liner.

At last the coastline of England came into sight; some time during the next day they would be docking. Bella was preparing for bed, thankful that the long voyage was almost at an end, when there was a knock on her cabin door.

She opened it to Resaldar. He said formally—'May I come in? There is something which I must discuss with you, and tonight is probably the last opportunity I shall have of speaking to you alone.'

She reached for a shawl with which to cover her nightgown, and sat down on the bunk. 'What is it, Resaldar?'

He hesitated for a moment, and then seated himself beside her, taking care that they should not touch.

'You said,' he began, 'that you would send Mr Munday, the lawyer, a telegram as soon as we have docked, asking him to meet us in London when our train arrives.'

'Yes.'

Resaldar looked down at his hands. 'You told me there are places in London, called inns and hostelries, where one may put up indefinitely.'

'That is so,' Bella confirmed, puzzled. 'Why?'

'I intend asking Mr Munday to arrange for you and Simon to stay at such a place at my expense.'

'But—I don't understand—'

A stark note entered his voice. 'I—cannot contemplate living under the same roof with you at Haverington Hall, Arabella. I know it is your home, but—it is too much to ask.

'So, I propose that I should buy a property for you and Simon to share as soon as it may be arranged. It will be a long way from Haverington Hall, so that we would be unable to meet often. And I shall, of course, make myself responsible for Simon's education and his future. As for yourself—'

He broke off, and looked deep into her eyes. 'You will never want for anything.'

'*Won't I?*' There was desolation in her voice.

'Oh, my love . . .' Suddenly she was in his arms, his mouth at the hollow of her throat, his hands caressing and exploring her body. A great tide of longing and desire thundered through her and she moved under his hands, making it easier for him to untie the fastenings of her nightgown. She felt his mouth on her breasts and her body gave a long shudder of response.

Someone knocked on the cabin door, shocking them both into sanity. Bella had scarcely had time to sit up and draw the shawl over her disarranged gown before the door opened and Fawzia entered.

Bella's face flamed. But she ought to have remembered that Fawzia belonged to a culture where women were expected to share their men, for there was no jealousy or suspicion on the girl's face.

'Oh, I am glad to find you here, Resaldar Khan!' she exclaimed with relief. 'I could not seek you out in the troops' quarters, and so I meant to ask Bella to speak to you on my behalf—'

'Sit down, Fawzia,' Resaldar said, making room for her on the bunk. 'What do you wish to speak to me about?'

Fawzia gave him a supplicating look. 'I have become friendly with Sister Augusta during the voyage, Resaldar Khan. She has been granted home leave from her duties in India, but because she has no family of her own left she had intended to spend her time in England in what she calls a convent. I—I wondered whether she might be invited to stay at this Haverington Hall instead.'

'But of course, my dear Fawzia!'

She clasped her hands in front of her in an ingrained

gesture of humble thanks. 'That is kind of you, Resaldar Khan. I shall go and tell her now.'

When she had left the cabin, Bella said slowly— 'Resaldar, your plans are not practical. You know nothing of Haverington Hall, of the estate, of the nearby village. *I* do. And I can imagine the effect it will have if you arrive there alone with Fawzia and a Catholic nun.'

His head went up, and his blue eyes were those of the arrogant Khan of Shapoora, Pretender to the throne of Kabul. 'I care nothing for the effect we may create—'

'You would be made to care, if not on your own behalf, then on Fawzia's. The people of Haverington have never before seen anyone of her race and colour, and she would not be accepted unless I helped to ease her into the community.' Bella gave a bleak little laugh. 'Believe me, whether you like it or not, you need me, Resaldar.'

He sighed, and rose. 'Yes, I need you in more ways than you can possibly imagine. Very well; if it is necessary for you to accompany us to Haverington Hall, then I submit.'

At the door he turned and added harshly, 'I trust Haverington Hall is large enough to enable you and me to meet as seldom as possible!'

CHAPTER
TWELVE

THE ONE thing Bella had failed to take into consideration
was the fact that Britain would be in the grip of winter by
the time they arrived. So much had happened since she
and Simon had left that she had lost track of the seasons.

She herself, fortunately, possessed the warm worsted
gown and cloak in which she had begun her travels, and
Simon, too, had adequate protection against the cold.
Presumably Sister Augusta wore layers of woollen
underclothing beneath her habit, for she seemed inured
to the elements. Fawzia and Resaldar, however, had
perforce to wear the outer coverings issued to them by
the Army in Afghanistan after they had disembarked
and were making for the station to catch the London
train.

Resaldar looked quite regal with his tall figure enveloped in the *choga*, a soft, warm cloak made of camel's
hair. But Fawzia's alien quality was emphasised by the
poshteen which she wore over the drab, slate-grey gown
which she had chosen in Bombay. The *poshteen* was a
garment made of sheepskin, and when worn by scouts in
its natural element of Afghanistan it seemed quite ordinary. On Fawzia, it looked incongruous and outlandish
in the murk of an English winter.

Both she and Resaldar had already gained some
notion of what Western civilization was like on the train
through India and during their brief stay in Bombay, so

that the rail journey to London did not make too startling an impact on them. The countryside was shrouded
in fog, so that little of it could be seen.

But London must have come as a deep shock to
both of them, even though Resaldar concealed his
reaction carefully. Mr Munday was waiting for them
on the platform, and after introductions had been
completed he whisked them away in his carriage to a
nearby inn.

Fawzia, shivering even inside her *poshteen*, was clearly bewildered by the yellow, sulphurous light which the
gas lamps cast over the streets, and terrified by the size of
the milling crowds. Bella had noticed her deep shock,
too, at the sight of painted young women blatantly
offering themselves to soldiers as they spilled from the
train.

They ate supper in the private parlour of the inn, and
immediately afterwards Fawzia and Sister Augusta excused themselves and retired to bed. Simon yawned and
announced that he, too, intended turning in. Bella knew
that Mr Munday had a good deal which he would need to
discuss with Resaldar, and she rose.

'I shall leave you two alone.'

Mr Munday escorted her to the door. In a low
voice, he said, 'I had intended suggesting that you
should remain for a few days in London, and take Mr
Haverington's fiancée shopping. But—'

'Yes, I know,' Bella murmured. 'I think Fawzia had
better be introduced to London very gradually, and over
an extended period of time. Besides, for the moment she
will be happier with the few simple, plain gowns which
were bought for her in Bombay.'

Mr Munday nodded. 'I shall place my carriage at your
disposal in the morning, and follow later in a hired
conveyance.' He added inconsequentially, and with

relief in his voice, 'John Haverington, at least, should fit in well enough.'

It was still impossible for Bella to think of Resaldar as John Haverington, and she had to make a conscious effort to do so.

Early the next morning, after breakfast, they set off in Mr Munday's carriage for Haverington Hall. The fog had lifted, but a fine, misty drizzle cloaked the country-side in a depressing pall as the carriage travelled through it.

Bella glanced at Fawzia, sitting beside Sister Augusta. She could not help wishing that Resaldar had consulted her before allowing the nun to be invited to the Hall at this particular time. He could not know, as she did, the deep distrust with which the staunchly Protestant villagers and estate workers regarded what they called Popery.

In itself, and coming at a different time, Sister Augusta's visit would not have caused too much com-ment. But taken in conjunction with Fawzia's obvious foreign looks and manners, her arrival would throw everyone into a state of further confusion and dismay.

Bella sighed. Great-Uncle Howard, in spite of his unpleasant manner and his general unpopularity, had nevertheless been one of *them*. A future mistress of the Hall who was foreign, with a dusky skin and slanting eyes, and whose best friend appeared to be a nun, would be a different matter altogether.

Bella glanced at Resaldar, carefully making her ex-pression neutral. 'What do you think of England so far?'

'I think it is very green and damp, and I regret that there are no mountains hereabouts.'

'But there are no bandits either,' Simon put in. He might have intended the remark to be a consolation, but there was a distinct note of regret in his voice.

It had not escaped Resaldar, who smiled. 'Yes, I suspect life might be somewhat dull here.'

'Oh, it is not dull at all!' This time there was conviction in Simon's voice. 'There is hunting and shooting, and Haverington offers some of the finest fishing in the county!'

Resaldar made no reply, but Fawzia asked in a puzzled voice, 'Why do the English grow so many dead trees?'

Simon glanced out of the window, and then threw back his head with laughter. 'That is an apple orchard, and the trees are not dead! They have merely lost their leaves for the winter!'

'We are approaching Haverington Hall now,' Bella announced.

Resaldar stared out of the carriage window as the Hall appeared in view. If he were impressed, he did not show it.

Mr Munday had recalled all the servants and they were lined up outside the front entrance as the carriage entered the drive and came to a halt.

Resaldar stepped from the vehicle and held out his hand to Fawzia. It was clear, from his manner, that he meant to ignore the servants, but that he expected some gesture of respect from them at the same time.

Bella laid a restraining hand on his arm. 'You have to meet all the servants, Resaldar.'

'*Meet* them?' His amazement matched his natural arrogance.

Halfway between anger and amusement, Bella explained, 'This is not Shapoora, Resaldar! You do not ignore your servants, or expect them to salaam to you! Now come, let me introduce you and Fawzia to them.'

Her heart sank when she saw the stunned disbelief

with which the servants received the news that Fawzia
was betrothed to the new master of Haverington Hall.

They accepted *him* unreservedly; he was Great-Uncle
Howard's grandson and in spite of the *choga* he looked
as British as they did themselves. But this strange,
foreign dark girl in her drab gown and outlandish
sheepskin toga, and her inhibited air of humility, was
someone completely beyond their experience.

Bella could have hugged her young brother when she
heard him introducing Sister Augusta to the servants in
their wake. 'The Sister is a nurse who has been caring for
our wounded soldiers out in India,' he explained, 'and
because she needs a rest after all she has been through,
we have invited her to stay for a while.' Thus at least
one awkwardness had been smoothed over. There
were murmurs of sympathy from the servants; Sister
Augusta's connection with Popery were overlooked
and she was accepted as a more than deserving case for
the Hall's hospitality.

As they stepped inside, Bella tried to see everything
through Resaldar's eyes. The wide entrance hall with the
circular staircase sweeping upwards to the gallery, along
whose walls hung portraits of Haverington ancestors;
then the drawing room with its two fireplaces, its carved
giltwood tables and its suite of walnut settees, its ornate
mirrors and its ormolu clocks.

She guided them through to the morning room whose
walls were hung with 17th century tapestries. She
pointed out the marquetry cabinets housing the family
collection of Meissen porcelain, and the writing table of
beech wood entirely overlaid with a veneer of gleaming
brass and tortoiseshell, and which was said to have been
made by Boulle, cabinet-maker to Louis XIV.

Resaldar's expression remained completely neutral.
Bella thought of his mud-walled residence in the village

of Shapoora, and of the stark contrast which it formed with the Hall. Was Resaldar passionately wishing himself back in his sun-baked kingdom instead?

On reflection, she decided it was far more likely that he was telling himself, *I am the grandson of an Emir. Why should I be over-awed by all this, when but for cruel fate I could have resided in the* Bala Hissar *with all its opulence and splendour?*

She suppressed a sigh. 'Perhaps I had better show you to your rooms now. Luncheon will shortly be served, and you will wish to freshen up before then.'

Everyone followed her along the winding staircase. The bedrooms had been aired and a fire was burning in each. Bella said with difficulty, 'Resaldar, you are to have the master bedroom which Fawzia will share with you after your marriage.'

He nodded, his expression stony, and Bella did not linger after she had opened the door of the room for him.

Fawzia, as befitting her status of future mistress of the Hall, had been given the principal guest room which possessed a smaller, adjoining room intended for the use of a personal maid.

But Fawzia seemed to shrink as she stood just inside the door of the room with its splendidly draped four-poster and its frivolously feminine furnishings.

'It—it is so large and so strange,' she muttered. 'I wondered—if Sister Augusta would not object, whether we might share it?'

'Poor child,' the nun said, placing a protective arm about Fawzia's shoulder. 'I would gladly sleep in the adjoining room. It must all seem very frightening and alien to you.'

The matter was settled, and Bella found herself alone in the corridor with Simon. Her brother had matured a good deal during their adventures, for he said with unexpected insight, 'Things are going to be very difficult for a while.'

'Yes.' Bella rubbed a tired hand over her forehead. 'Simon, it is too late in the term to make it worthwhile for you to return to school, and you are desperately needed here. Would you show Resaldar around the estate, and explain how things are run, and—and tactfully try to suppress any signs he might show of reverting to his role as the Khan of Shapoora?'

'Don't worry, Sis.' Simon hugged her briefly. 'I know precisely what you mean. I'll school Resaldar while you educate Fawzia. I fancy your task promises to be far, far more difficult than mine.'

His prophecy proved to be only too accurate. Outwardly, at least, Resaldar made the transition to John Haverington fairly quickly and with little difficulty, and established a favourable relationship with the estate manager and the workers and tenant farmers.

Fawzia was a different matter, however. She shrank from the role of future mistress of Haverington Hall and she was as frightened of the servants as they were wary and uncomfortable with her. She only appeared to be happy when she and Sister Augusta were deep in discussion of some theological subject or other.

Each Sunday she attended services in the private chapel whose minister received a stipend from the estate, and the same curate called daily to instruct her in the Catechism. Once she had been confirmed, she and Resaldar would announce their marriage. But although Fawzia applied herself dutifully to the curate's instruction, she could not disguise her lack of enthusiasm.

In the meantime, Bella was aware that their neighbours were becoming increasingly curious about the new master of Haverington Hall and his future bride. They had all left their cards at the Hall, and Bella had set out to return their calls, explaining that John Haverington and his fiancée needed a little time to adjust to their new surroundings.

But the neighbours could not be fobbed off forever, and when Bella learnt that the Ransomes planned a ball to which everyone in the district were to be invited, she decided that she would *have* to take the initiative and arrange an earlier dinner party at which Fawzia could be presented to everyone on her home ground. To be plunged straight into a country ball in a strange house would terrify the poor girl.

Bella and Resaldar had been making conscious efforts to avoid being alone with one another, but on this occasion she was forced to seek him out and discuss the matter with him.

He heard her out, and then nodded, his expression bleak. 'Try to make matters as easy as possible for Fawzia, will you?'

'Of course. The first thing I intend doing is sending for a seamstress, so that a suitable gown may be made for her.'

Resaldar glanced at her, and looked away. 'I have learnt enough of Western civilization to realise that *your* gowns are not very suitable either. Commission one for yourself as well, but—but not like the one—.'

He stopped. She knew precisely what he had meant. Her gown must not in any way remind him of the gold Surah silk trimmed with Breton lace which had belonged to Nicolette, and which might bring desperately suppressed passions to dangerous flash-point.

Bella sent for a seamstress from the village that same morning, and she arrived with her pattern book. Fawzia was deep in conversation with Sister Augusta in the rooms which they shared, and Bella decided not to disturb her yet. She herself was better qualified to choose the styles, and Fawzia need only be brought in afterwards to approve her choice and enable the seamstress to take her measurements.

Bella gave herself up to the totally female thrill of choosing new clothes. For herself, she settled upon a charming sketch of a pale-blue *pékin* foundation, designed to be worn underneath a gown made up of different fabrics and colours. The front of the bodice, cut low and square, was of fluted white silk edged with a quilling of white gauze and lace, descending to a point at the waist. The skirt was of Pompadour brocade with a blue ground and a pattern of vari-coloured flowers, with paniers on the hips, and the sleeves were finished with three frills of lace caught up with a blue bow.

For Fawzia, she picked out a pretty gown of white satin cut in the princess style, with a low bodice trimmed with a band of brocade, short sleeves and a flounced skirt. The only decoration was a wreath of artificial flowers stitched from one shoulder to the hip. Both Bella and the seamstress agreed that it was demure and youthful and just right for a girl's first formal gown.

When Fawzia was called in to approve the choice, however, they were stunned by her reaction. The seamstress listened, open-mouthed, as Fawzia protested that she could not possibly wear such an immodest, ornate gown. It was the first time the seamstress had clapped eyes on Fawzia, and both the girl's looks and her protestations made the woman stare at her as if she were a being from a different planet.

Biting her lower lip, Bella tried to save the situation. 'Look through the pattern book yourself, Fawzia, and see if there is anything else you would rather choose.'

Her choice stunned Bella as much as it did the seamstress. 'Begging your pardon, Miss,' the latter told

Fawzia, 'but what you've picked out is a mourning gown.'

'Is it? What is a mourning gown? *I* think it would be most suitable.'

'A mourning gown,' Bella explained gently, 'is what one wears if someone in the family has died.'

'Well, it is the gown in which I would feel most comfortable,' Fawzia insisted.

Shaking her head, the seamstress took the girl's measurements, and when she had finished, Fawzia appealed to Bella, 'May I go now, please? Sister Augusta was in the middle of telling me about the most interesting case she was called upon to nurse in the field-hospital.'

Bella nodded, and when they were alone once more she told the seamstress, 'Make the gown of black velvet instead of crape, and don't cut the bodice quite so high at the neck.'

The seamstress made no comment as she collected her pattern book and her lists of measurements, but Bella knew it would be all over the district that the foreign girl who was to be the new mistress at Haverington Hall had chosen a mourning gown for her first formal social appearance.

The dinner party itself could not have been described as anything but a disaster. Resaldar, looking quite magnificent and completely at ease in his formal cut-away coat, narrow trousers and snow-white shirt topped with a silk cravat at the neck, glanced at Bella in her new gown and looked quickly away.

An expression of mingled anguish and pity flashed across his face as Fawzia descended the stairs in her sombre black. Even the fact that it had been fashioned of velvet could not disguise what it was, and she had draped a black silk fichu over her shoulders to disguise the fact that the bodice had been cut low.

The first of the guests began to arrive. They tried, politely, to hide their reaction at their initial meeting with Fawzia, and most of them made sincere attempts to draw her out as the evening progressed.

But she continued to wear a trapped, haunted look, and confined herself to answering questions put to her. To Bella, it was obvious that she wished only to escape to the room which she shared with Sister Augusta, and in which the nun was having her dinner served privately. It had been Sister Augusta's own wish not to be included in the dinner party.

After the meal, Bella led the ladies to the drawing room and left the men to their port, aware that their over-hearty banter was a disguise for the embarrassment they all felt on their host's behalf.

In the drawing room, the conversation among the ladies was so stilted, and Fawzia looked so uncomfortable that Bella said, after a while, 'I can see that you are not feeling well, Fawzia. One of your wretched headaches again, I daresay. I'm sure you will excuse us, ladies, if I see her to her room?'

Fawzia looked bewildered, grateful and close to tears as Bella escorted her from the room. Once outside, she began to weep. 'It—it was all perfectly awful . . .'

She was right, of course. But aloud, Bella said, 'Nonsense! You acquitted yourself quite well, and with practice you will become more used to our social ways.'

At this Fawzia only began to cry more bitterly, and Bella was glad to hand her over to the sympathetic Sister Augusta.

As she approached the drawing room again, she could hear the women talking, and snatches of their comments reached her.

'Quite unsuitable . . .'

'Whatever could young Haverington be thinking of?'

'. . . never fit in. One has to feel sorry for her, poor child, but still . . .'

The evening came to an early end. The guests were filled with embarrassed pity for their hosts, and they were also eager to hold an inquest on the strange choice young Haverington had made in betrothing himself to a foreign girl who wore a mourning gown to her own dinner party, and then disappeared from it on a fabricated excuse.

Depressed, Bella went to her room. She removed her beautiful new gown carefully and put on her nightshift, and sat down by the dressing table to brush her hair. In the looking glass, she saw her door being opened, and she turned in her chair.

'I have come to say goodbye,' Resaldar told her in a stark voice.

She rose slowly, and went to him. He had removed his coat and his cravat and she saw that his hair was disordered. He had also quite clearly continued drinking since the departure of the guests. But if his intention had been to get drunk he had obviously failed. The anguish in his eyes made that quite plain.

'You—you are sending me away?' Bella whispered.

'No. I cannot subject Fawzia to so much that is alien to her, and which will always be alien to her. So—I am leaving in the morning, and taking her with me.'

'You cannot return to Afghanistan, Resaldar!' Bella cried. 'You know that you will always be in danger there from your cousins and uncles!'

He gave her a twisted smile. 'Yes. So I shall go to India instead. I shall apply for some kind of clerical post. I shall convert to Islam so that Fawzia need not abandon her faith.'

'You—you cannot make such a sacrifice for someone you do not even love . . .' Bella muttered.

'Why not? *She* has been trying very hard to make equal sacrifices for me.'

'Oh, Resaldar . . .'

He reached blindly for her, and drew her against him. Her mouth opened beneath his as their lips met and her entire body was alive with a desperate hunger for him. She began to unbutton his shirt, moving her fingers over his flesh.

'Stay with me,' she whispered. 'Let me have tonight . . .'

He made a groaning sound and shook his head, releasing her.

'Please . . .'

'No, Arabella. Fawzia is still awake; I could hear voices coming from her room. I wish to tell her my decision and put her out of her misery. But I don't know whether they are in a state of undress or not. Will you go and find out for me?'

Feeling numb and defeated, Bella moved with leaden steps and found a robe which she belted about her waist. 'Wait in the corridor,' she told Resaldar dully.

When she knocked on the door of their adjoining rooms, it was opened to her by Sister Augusta. She was fully dressed.

'I am sorry to disturb you, Sister,' Bella said, 'but Mr Haverington wishes to talk to Fawzia. Where is she?'

'At the moment she is at prayer in my room. But ask Mr Haverington to come inside. There is something I wish to say to him, also.'

Mystified, Bella turned and beckoned to Resaldar. She noticed that the door of the adjoining room was firmly closed while Fawzia prayed—to God, or to Allah?

Sister Augusta asked Bella and Resaldar to sit down.

The room was furnished with several armchairs, and all three of them took a seat. The nun twisted the gold band upon her finger and began to speak, her eyes fixed on Resaldar's face.

'Mr Haverington, I should like to assure you that, however things may appear to you, I have not deliberately abused your hospitality—'

'*Abused?*' He frowned at her in bewilderment.

'From the beginning, there has been an affinity between myself and Fawzia,' the nun went on. 'She was interested in all the facets of my religion, and in the Order to which I belong. We have had many theological discussions—'

'Yes, I am aware of that.'

'This evening was extremely upsetting for her. She knew that she did not fit in, that she would never fit in, and it was not only because she is a foreigner in a strange land. It is because she cannot come to terms with the material side of life. She cannot find happiness in ordinary social activities.'

Sister Augusta glanced at Bella. 'When you brought her to me in tears, she told me that she had been thinking for quite a while now about the matter of converting from Islam to Christianity. But she is not drawn to the Protestant creed. She wishes to become a Catholic instead, and tonight finally decided her.

'We intended telling you in the morning that she wishes to leave with me, and enter a convent where she may study and eventually take her vows.'

Resaldar shook his head. 'I do not blame you in any way, Sister, and I believe you when you say that you did nothing to influence her actively. But she is merely using Catholicism as an escape. Do you think I have been blind to her unhappiness?'

At that moment the door of the adjoining room

opened, and Fawzia appeared. Resaldar rose, and went to her, taking her gently by the hand.

'Come and sit down, Fawzia. Sister Augusta has been telling me about the decision you have reached. But there is no need for you to do any such thing. I have made up my mind to take you back—not to Afghanistan, but to India, where you may practise your faith, and where we shall be married according to the rites of Islam—'

'Resaldar Khan,' Fawzia interrupted quietly, 'I do indeed wish to go to India, but not in the circumstances which you have described. I want to join the Order to which Sister Augusta belongs, and give my life in service to others.'

'I cannot believe that you would willingly abandon Islam, when it meant so much to you!' Resaldar exclaimed.

Fawzia smiled. 'To be honest, it was the rites and the ceremonies of Islam to which I was clinging. Your own Protestant faith seemed so casual and matter-of-fact by contrast. The Order to which Sister Augusta belongs practise quite as many sacraments and rites as does Islam, but that is not why I wish to convert. I want to serve God, and nurse the sick and the dying. I do not want to spend my life in giving dinner parties and wearing frivolous gowns.'

'I am beginning to believe that you really do mean all this,' Resaldar said slowly.

'Oh, I do!' Anxiety entered Fawzia's eyes. 'The only thing is, Resaldar Khan, that you will be required to release me from my vow to be your wife. For if you will not, I cannot enter the Order.'

He touched her forehead lightly with his fingers. 'I gladly release you, my dear.'

'Oh, you are so good, so generous!' She smiled tentatively at him. 'I know you said that you did not wish to marry Bella, Resaldar Khan. But a man needs a wife, and I would feel much relieved in my mind if you would consider it.'

'I shall certainly give it thought,' he said gravely.

'I believe,' Fawzia added reflectively, 'that Bella wishes very much to marry *you*, Resaldar Khan.'

'I believe you may be right, my dear. She and I will leave you now, so that we may discuss it.'

He rose, and held out his hand to Bella. Her mind was spinning and her heart was racing as he drew her into the corridor. She found that he was leading her very deliberately towards his own master bedroom.

Bella hung back as he opened the door. 'Resaldar, no—'

'This room,' he interrupted harshly, 'has become haunted for me by thoughts of sharing it with Fawzia instead of with you. I need you to help me exorcise the ghosts.'

'I—we must not—'

'No more than half an hour ago,' he reminded her, his eyes filled with laughter now, 'you were trying to seduce me into staying with you for the night. Very well, my dearest Arabella; I am as clay in your hands. Seduce me to your heart's content!'

He moved to the bed and sat on its edge, his eyes challenging her but his mouth soft with love and longing.

She moved towards him, and knelt on the floor. Experimentally, she kissed his lips, and felt his mouth open invitingly, demandingly, under hers.

She took his hands in hers, and he allowed himself to be brought to his feet. Slowly and solemnly, she began to undress him, moving her mouth over his body, caressing it with her tongue, so that a deep sound rose in his throat.

She paused to slip her nightshift over her head, and allowed it to fall on the floor. Then he pulled her down beside him on the bed and time became suspended as their naked bodies melted together.

He parted her thighs gently, mindful of her lack of experience, and the sudden sharp pain was almost immediately forgotten in the growing, urgent excitement which filled her as she yielded and moved against him until the final simultaneous explosion of ecstasy engulfed both of them.

Afterwards, she stared intently into his eyes. They were soft with remembered delight, and he touched her mouth with the tips of his fingers.

'I love you,' he said, 'and I want to marry you as soon as possible.'

She was unable to answer, her heart too filled with emotion.

He laughed softly, and said with mock-horror, 'Could Fawzia possibly have been wrong? Having had your evil way with me, are you now giving me to understand that you do not wish to marry me after all?'

She leant over him, and laid her mouth on his, and mutely confirmed the answer which he had been sure of for a long, long time.

The perfect holiday romance.